Legs Eleven

By Sarah May Fraser

For my family and friends. Thanks for putting up with my constant stream of hopes and dreams. xxx

PROLOGUE

Mari picked up a magazine from the oak desk and fanned her hot face with it.

"Calm down, Mar," said Louisa as she tugged on the corset ribbons from behind.

"Not too tight!" barked her sister with a cherry-red stress complexion.

"It needs to be tight to boost up that bust," Louisa insisted through gritted teeth. "Just breathe slowly, look at the mood board and think: 'I am a seductress. I am not in my normal life. This is.... an escape'."

Louisa grinned at her sister, hoping to transfer some false confidence across and into Mari's trembling bones.

Mari exhaled slowly, glancing at her reflection in the mirror. The black and purple satin corset nipped her in at the waist, and her cleavage... well, she had never before seen it stacked so... welcomingly. She looked over at the mood board Louisa had placed on the desk as a last-minute inspiration top-up. Vintage pin-up girls pouted and posed between cuttings of lace and ribbon, making Mari feel no less nervous.

An assistant, who clutched her clipboard as if the entire evening would erupt in chaos if she so much as laid it down for a second, popped her head in the room and bleated: "You're on in five minutes".

"Just for tonight," said Louisa, suddenly coming over all serious, "you are Legs Eleven."

Mari's stomach lurched. She nodded in agreement. Fear and agreement.

CHAPTER ONE

Five months earlier....

Louisa lay beneath the thin white bed sheet, sullen and motionless. Sun light washed through the apartment and the sounds of the city drifted up and through the open windows to her lonesome spot on the tenth floor.

Fans whirred in each corner of the room, not really cooling her down, just wafting the warm air around.

The left side of the bed was neat – the pillows untouched. Louisa curled her long legs round to her front, almost forming the foetal position, with the side of her head sinking into the puffy white pillow. She held her hand in front of her delicate, pretty face and examined the diamond on her ring finger sadly.

Justin had picked it out in secret before proposing on a yacht, boasting of its four-figure value as he slid it on her finger.

Life in Dubai had been as though her former life in Scotland had been turned on its head, pumped full of cash and washed over with warm sunshine. But all this was coming to an end. Justin wanted her out by the time he returned from a business trip in four days' time.

Never being one to organise her own affairs, she had simply asked, desperately, and with a touch of sarcasm: "How am I supposed to do that? Do you want me to just pack up all this stuff and book a flight to Scotland?"

"Exactly," had been his stern reply before he slammed the front door on his way out.

Her mobile buzzed on the bedside table. She slowly turned over to read a text message, tossing her long dark hair away from her face.

"Hi babe, you coming over for cocktails and sewing? I've got some hems I need help with. I'll pay you in booze, and massages – I've hired the spa guys to come round."

It was one of The Wives. The partners of all Justin's colleagues had formed a social group of thin, beautiful ladies of leisure with a real talent for spending cash.

"Not today," she replied, then slumped forward and slowly rose out of bed.

It was pushing thirty degrees Celsius and she felt hot even in her light satin vest and knickers. She sauntered through to the large open plan kitchen and sitting area, which gleamed and sparkled with recessed spotlights and marble. Louisa had never cleaned the apartment, of course. There were people to do that for her.

She took a sip from a carton of pomegranate juice from the fridge before resting her elbows on the counter and burying her face in her hands.

"You total bitch loser," she hissed. "You selfish, waste of space, horrible person. You've screwed things up, yet again. Well done. Really, really, well done."

There was a light tap on the main door out to the lifts – or elevators, as everyone around here seemed to call them.

Louisa strode over to look through the peep hole. A caretaker wearing a pale blue polo shirt stood anxiously. He was young, with perfect olive skin and jet black hair.

"Go away!" she yelled. "I'm leaving tomorrow."

After a few seconds of silence, she peered through the peephole again to see the caretaker resting his head against the wall to the side of the door, with his arm above his head, looking down to the ground. He was chanting or whispering something desperately.

Louisa turned the chrome door handle and tentatively pulled open the door.

She locked eyes with the caretaker. He walked gently towards her in silence, his eyes glued to hers the whole time. Louisa moved to the side, allowing him to pass her and enter the apartment. The door swung shut with a bang.

CHAPTER TWO

Mari tapped the mouse abruptly and groaned inwardly to open yet another customer complaint email. Her role as administrator for Williamson and Son Furniture had expanded gradually in the six years she had been there until suddenly she seemed to be accountable for the lot – complaints, marketing, customer databases, hiring delivery firms, collecting drums of disgusting instant coffee (or sawdust, as she joked) from the wholesale store down the road and even fetching the staff elevenses. None of this had been hinted at when she was first hired by sleazy Steve, daddy Williamson. She loathed it when he pronounced her name "Mareee", despite her explaining: "It's pronounced Marry, as in 'Marry me'." "OK," he had responded with a seedy little laugh, disappointed no-one had been around to hear.

Mari often caught Steve casting his eyes down her shapely figure during another one of his pleas for her to work overtime. At thirty-two, Mari was attractive, but not stunning. She had all the ingredients to be a belter of a dame, if she wanted, but she just didn't know how to use them to their fullest. Her hair, usually scraped back into a ponytail, was a luscious brown and because she rarely tampered with hair colours and products it was as silky as a ten-year-old's. Her pale blue eyes were hidden under green, plastic framed glasses, which, to be fair were quite trendy. Her complexion was clear and smooth, envied by her friends and her only real vice was a few too many bottles of wine during the week. She often snuck out to the glass recycling box outside the modern block of flats she lived in, holding them in a plastic bag for life steadily against her hip to avoid the tell-tale clinking of glass for all her neighbours to hear... again. It was a peaceful suburb of Inverness, where row upon row of newly built white homes had just recently sprung up, like spring daffodils. Mari, being sensible, had opted for a shared ownership, first time buyers' scheme to buy her flat and escape the city centre with its buses and pub punters disturbing her sleep.

Smart and reasonably pretty, Mari was getting used to the patronising script performed regularly by her mum and aunt, which went along the lines of: "You're such a good catch Mar, you need to show yourself off a bit more. Get some cleavage out, take the specs off and for goodness sake get some make-up on. Men would fall at your heels if you wanted them to."

And she did want them to, in a way.

Mari had always pictured that by her thirties she would be married with a couple of kids, not single, in a job she hated and permanently frustrated and not knowing how to get to where she wanted to be.

Once every couple of months she typed and tore up her resignation letter, angry at the dismissal of her talents. She had a degree in business and marketing, yet more often than not, the most valuable task she would perform in a day would be to queue up at the hot food van in the retail park car park, with a list of eight different requests, ranging from bacon roll with ketchup to burger with onions, no cheese. She felt like a mug and wanted out of there.

There was one thing holding her back from finally quitting, however, and that was Johnny.

Johnny was part of the "and sons" in Williamson and sons. He had the same roving eye as his father, yet somehow the way he devoured Mari's appearance, visually, felt more like validation than perversion.

He only joined the family firm a year before, having been an events co-ordinator in Greece for the best part of ten years.

"More like, getting pissed, shagging birds and begging old dad here for rent money," was how Steve had described it.

Mari wrote Johnny off as bad news the moment she met him, especially after his less than glowing reference from daddy. She saw him flirting on the shop floor with female customers, even when their husbands were lurking in the background and every Saturday girl went weak at the knees when he reeled off tales of drunken dilemmas lived out in his sunshine years.

He was twenty-eight – another reason she told herself not to get involved. Mari knew a toy boy was not what she needed. The clock was ticking, she believed. If babies were to be in her plan, she needed to meet a sensible, mature man soon – really soon, and get her plan underway.

She'd tried online dating and endured a couple of dinner dates with the sort of men she thought she wanted, but it never felt right. There was Tony the accountant who spoke endlessly about his mother, Derek the school janitor who asked her out on a second date to the local football ground for a pie – which never happened - and Brian, a supermarket sales assistant who was a mature student and showed promise, but never called her back after they spent the night together. Mari cursed herself for taking him home after the first date. She made a mental note to always hold back a bit after that. It had been her first sexual encounter in years, too, which made the rejection sting like a fresh graze rubbed with disinfectant.

For the first few months working with Johnny, Mari had been able to brush off his charm, seeing straight through it but Brenda's leaving do had been a game changer.

Not a huge party-goer, Mari almost never went to the party – a finger buffet in a soulless chain pub - but Brenda had been one of the nicer sales staff so she felt duty-bound to show support.

It was the first time anyone from work had seen her in a dress, albeit a loose dress which hid her curves. It was deep blue with three-quarter length sleeves and a high neckline, leaving *everything* to the imagination. It was also the first time they saw her without her glasses and a smudge of make-up on. She felt quite sexy that night, wearing her best control pants for a flatter stomach and some black high heels.

After several sickly sweet pitchers of cheap cocktails the laughter between the nine who had turned up was flowing and the night was at its peak of fun.

Johnny pulled up a seat next to Mari, who was grinning away as she listened to everyone exchanging stories about dreadful customers. That was Mari's way – happy on the outskirts of a group.

"You scrub up well," he commented, causing her to blush and take a sip with her straw at a loss for words. He smelled great, of a heavy aftershave, and had on a tight-fitted short-sleeved shirt, which showed off his muscular arms.

A few drinks later, when Mari was coming back from the loo, Johnny casually slipped his hand in hers and guided her outside and over to the bin shelter, away from prying eyes. Without asking he began kissing her. The shock rendered Mari motionless, and initial thoughts of: "how dare he just assume I want this," began to bubble inside her, but then the alcohol, plus the fact it had been so long since anyone had made her feel desirable, extinguished any negativity and she went with the gentle, warm flow.

The ten-minute snog session was interrupted by a small gaggle of the youngest sales assistants from Williamson's who were leaving to find a club. On hearing them discussing taxis, Johnny pulled away and said, whilst stroking Mari's waist and bottom: "I'd better go. My carriage awaits," then joined the group.

It looked a little pathetic, Johnny surrounding himself with youngsters, perching his arms on the shoulders of the stockroom boys.

Mari wiped her lipstick-stained mouth and left for home, feeling a mixture of thrill and embarrassment.

Weeks passed before Mari's next encounter with Johnny at work. She had seen him several times in passing, but he had behaved as if nothing had happened. It wasn't until they were alone in the tearoom one Wednesday afternoon that he acknowledged her.

"What you up to on Saturday?" he asked, with a slight sneer of arrogance.

"Nothing," replied Mari a little too eagerly and inwardly chastised herself.

"Fancy getting together?"

It was completely out of the blue. They hadn't even made small talk. Mari asked herself if this was normal or suspicious behaviour, she wasn't sure. A few moments of panicked hesitation passed as Mari tried to form her answer.

"Don't sweat it," Johnny offered with a laugh.

"No, I mean, yes, that could be good," Mari replied with an attempt at an assured smile.

She fancied him, really fancied him, and there was little else going on in her life, so why not, she reasoned.

This was to be the beginning of her on-off relationship with Johnny. He called her once a fortnight when he needed her. Well, needed her body.

She regularly made attempts to spend Sundays with him, suggesting walks on Ness Islands in the city centre or trips to the cinema, but he always came up with an excuse.

She was constantly suspicious of why someone so confident and good looking would be interested in someone like her - someone who, as she saw it, blended into the background.

She shyly questioned him occasionally on his flirtatious sales patter, which seemed to be getting worse now that she was seeing him, and he dismissed it as his "selling style".

"Women will pay more for a slightly better dining table if you make them feel good about themselves," he smugly revealed. "The amount of times I've added an extra fifty quid onto my bonus, just by giving someone's Mrs a sex-stare."

This sort of talk disgusted Mari, but she felt naively reassured to think it was all an act. Maybe it was all bravado, and like he had promised, he wasn't interested in actually being with anyone other than Mari.

One evening Johnny announced, over pasta at Mari's flat, that he thought they should be exclusive to each other.

"I thought we were," was Mari's shocked response.

"Oh, yes," Johnny agreed with a flustered tone, "we already are, I just mean, in official terms, so we know where we stand."

With that, he raised his glass and Mari feigned a smile and clinked hers to his. She made a conscious decision to see that as a positive step forward, rather than worry about what their relationship had, or hadn't, been up until that point.

Mari was beginning to settle into feeling happy with Johnny. She told her family and friends she had a boyfriend, which felt strangely immature to say at thirty-two. There were cries of: "I knew it! I said to your dad that you were getting some attention, because you've been wearing more make-up lately and you had on those tight jeans," from her mother, and "when can we meet him?" from her friend Steph.

Her sister, Louisa, texted: "About time, sis. Can't wait to meet him. I'm moving home, so we'll catch up then."

Of all the responses, that one was the one that floored her most. Louisa, back in her life. That was a mixed fortune.

CHAPTER THREE

The family sipped coffee from paper cups, perching on hard metal benches inside Inverness Airport.

Mari blew into her cup, watching the steam roll off, thinking about the storm that was brewing - that storm being the inevitable emotional flurry in which Louisa would sweep into arrivals.

Mum, Nancy, and dad, Bill, chatted casually about the garden and which pots needed attention before summer.

"Are you excited to see your little sister?" Nancy asked enthusiastically, as if Mari was still nine years old.

"Yeah. It's just a shame it has to be because there's yet more drama," she responded with huge restraint.

"I know, poor lass," chipped in Bill. "If I could get my hands on that Justin..." he trailed off, knowing that in reality he was as soft as a sponge cake.

"I can't believe there's no wedding to plan now. I was really looking forward to it," added Nancy.

Mari choked on her latte. Her parents hadn't been looking forward to the big event at all, as far as she had been aware. Justin's high-flying job in Dubai meant he had more cash in his back pocket than mum and dad had in their bank accounts. They had been scrimping and saving since the moment the dazzling engagement ring photo had been Facebooked by her sister six months previously. They cancelled a holiday to France, but begged Mari not to tell Louisa this fact.

"It'll spoil the celebrations," Nancy had hissed. "She mustn't know the stress this wedding is putting on our finances."

Of course not, thought Mari. *We mustn't upset the baby*.

The phone call from Dubai had come three days ago.

"Dad," sobbed Louisa, "I need to come home. It's over between me and Justin. He's throwing me out. I don't know what to do. I need you and mum."

Within minutes Bill had transferred the funds. He hadn't told Mari about this little detail. Stable, want-for-nothing Mari should not know that the bank of mum and dad had bailed her younger sister out yet again.

Suddenly passengers began to flow out of the exit from arrivals, dragging their huge wheeled suitcases wearily along the shiny, marble effect floor.

Nancy thrust her cup into Mari's spare hand and darted forward expectantly, clutching her hands together in anticipation.

Two chunky guys turned left and Louisa came into view. Her long wavy hair had been dyed darker, her lips were crimson and her long legs marched confidently like those of a cat-walk model beneath a patterned tea dress and denim jacket. Her chunky ankle boots added that extra element of cool she always seemed to manage. A smile burst across her face under enormous sun glasses.

Why the hell is she wearing shades in an airport? thought Mari, as she slowly rose from her seat, tossed the cups in a nearby bin and stood behind Nancy and Bill, who was now putting one arm around his wife's shoulders.

"My baby girl!" shrieked Nancy.

They giggled and hugged and Bill put his other arm protectively around his youngest daughter.

"Let's get you back home girl," he said in a gentle, reassuring tone.

"Hey Mari, you look....great," said Louisa, as if stuck for something deeper to say.

"You too," Mari replied offering a hollow hug with their bodies barely touching.

"Thanks for coming," Louisa said sincerely to her older sister.

"Mum thought you'd like it if we were all here."

Louisa gave a short sigh of disappointment at that answer and then switched on the charming smile once more.

"What are you still wearing that thing for?" asked her dad suddenly pointing at Louisa's engagement ring.

"Dad! It cost six grand! I'm not going to put it away in a box."

"Yes, yes," soothed Nancy, stroking her hair. "You're heartbroken. You can wear it as long as you like."

Louisa slid it from her wedding finger, eyeballing her dad, and swapped it to her right hand instead.

"Better?" she asked, not really looking for an answer.

The four McAllisters walked out of the airport, into the light spring rain – Bill covering Louisa with a huge golf umbrella all the way to their Ford Focus.

Mari trailed behind, as usual.

CHAPTER FOUR

Hot tomato sauce, bubbled furiously in a huge pan on the hob, like molten lava waiting to burst out of a volcano.

Whitney Houston's "I'm every woman" boomed from the Ipod docking station on the kitchen counter, competing with the high-pitched whirring of the food processor next to it.

Mari held one hand over the processor lid, which was cracked, whilst controlling the metallic power dial with the other. Pink pork mince, riddled with white fat blobs, raw eggs and bread had blended into a smooth, slimy paste - ready for forming into meatballs and baking.

After they turned a golden brown, Mari plopped them into the tomato sauce, placed the pan lid on top, washed her hands thoroughly, sniffed them for garlic, then washed them a bit more.

She took out a wine glass and unscrewed the lid of a half-empty bottle of chardonnay to fill a glass, two thirds of the way.

After a quick scan of her Ipod, wine glass in one hand, she settled for Jess Glynn – she was in the mood for something upbeat - and shimmied her way through the immaculate cream hallway to her bedroom.

The flat was minimalist, and not in a chic way. Mari's abode was bland. She, as a person, didn't feel bland, she just never knew which style belonged to her.

She opted for run-of-the-mill beach scene pre-framed pictures from Ikea for the bathroom, as that was a safe bet, and wicker-woven hearts for the bedroom wall, also safe. She occasionally lusted after extravagant ornaments in department stores, which would have placed an enormous "look at me and my vivacious personality" statement right in the middle of this beige box, but she just never had the nerve, or the spare cash, to do herself justice.

After a quick shower Mari pulled on a tight-fitting burgundy dress, left her shoulder-length hair down, for a change, and applied her make-up - in more bold tones than usual, including red lipstick - and stood in front of her full-length bedroom mirror to cautiously examine her appearance.

Her healthy figure, a shapely size 12 to 14, was displayed perfectly in the dress, like a painting brought to life by an elegant frame. But to Mari's ever critical eye it wasn't right. She sighed and groaned to see the dress hugging her bum tightly and she grabbed the small fleshy bulge above her knicker elastic with both hands and whimpered.

The phone in the hallway rang, and Mari immediately ceased her self-damnation and cantered along the soft carpet to lift the cordless handset.

"Hi darling," said her mother in her usual hurried tone.

"Hi mum, how are you?" Mari replied as she padded back through to the bedroom.

"Yep fine, fine, I was just ringing to see if you want to come round on Sunday for a family lunch."

"A family lunch? Is there a special occasion?"

"No, it's just I thought it would be lovely to have my two daughters together, now that your sister's home."

Mari sat down on the bed, rolling her eyes. "Fine, that sounds good. What time?"

"How about come for noon?"

"Perfect."

"What are you up to tonight?" asked Nancy with an over the top curiosity.

"I'm cooking for Johnny," Mari said, and a smile tugged at the corners of her crimson lips.

"Ooh, lovely. Hey! Why don't you bring him on Sunday? We'd love to meet him."

Mari panicked, and stammered: "Er… I suppose I could ask him, but we haven't really done the whole family thing yet…"

"That's why I'm asking," interrupted Nancy. "Just get it over with."

"Ok, it's a bit short notice, but I'll ask him."

"Lovely. See you then, darling. Bye."

"Bye."

She glanced ahead at her reflection and tutted in disapproval. "I'm no Jessica Rabbit!"

A quick costume change later – into the blue shapeless dress she had worn the night she and Johnny first kissed – she returned to the open plan kitchen and

23

dining room and took two heart-shaped photo frames out of a plastic bag on the counter. She smiled to see a print of the selfie taken on her phone the week before at the pub. They looked happy. Johnny's chiselled jaw was emphasised by his grin and Mari was giggling so much at the time of the photo her eyes were half shut.

She carefully wrapped one frame in white paper with red hearts and placed it on the place mat in front of where Johnny would be sitting at the small square dining table, then placed the other frame on the book self in the corner of the room.

She poured another glass of wine and set about preparing the spaghetti.

The doorbell rang and Johnny walked in a second after it.

"Hi gorgeous," he exclaimed with a bit of a slow fake Texan drawl, and grabbed her by the waist to pull her in for a hard kiss.

Those were the moments Mari cherished. That was when she felt she was truly his, and he was truly hers.

"Jesus!" he shouted suddenly and burst out laughing.

"What?" queried Mari, laughing nervously.

"What the hell is that?" he said, pointing to the heart picture on the shelf.

"I just did that today," she explained. "Do you like it?"

"It's a bit feckin' soppy," he said frowning.

Mari's back was to the dining table and she was able to grab the wrapped present and hide it behind her back. She made her way into the kitchen area and slid it into a drawer.

"Dinner's just about ready," she said brightly, concealing her annoyance.

"Good, I'm bloody starving," Johnny said with a grin. "I need to line my stomach properly."

"Steady on, I don't have *that* much wine in the flat, you won't be getting sozzled tonight," Mari commented with a laugh.

"Nah, babe, I mean for later. I'm meeting Keks and Tiny in town after dinner," he replied.

"Really?" Mari stood, glued to the spot with disbelief, with a plastic sieve in mid air. "You're not staying here tonight?"

She couldn't hide her disappointment this time.

"I thought I told you that," he said, unflinching. "It's Keks's last weekend before he goes back off shore to work for four weeks. I promised him a big night."

"Right. I guess I'll be watching The X Factor again then."

"Don't get all moody on me," he said lowering his face and smiling sweetly, almost pleadingly. "We'd maybe have time for a quick one before I leave." He made a loop with his finger and poked his forefinger in and out of it.

"That's not what I'm disappointed about!" She practically spat the words out. "I was hoping we could just chill out, have a few drinks, watch a movie... have a nice time."

"Next time," he said, downing his wine before glancing at the wall clock.

Dinner was served and they ate happily, albeit too quickly.

"Slow down," urged Mari. "If I've only got you for this meal, then at least make it pleasurable."

"Yes, mum," Johnny teased, winking.

Although his manners were pitiful and he always turned up empty-handed with nothing to contribute towards to meal, when he winked at her, or squeezed her bum, or did other similarly sexually-suggestive gestures, Mari softened to him. It was as though the outright maleness of his behaviour made her feel more girly. His cockiness made her feel lucky to have him.

After wolfing down his meal, Johnny sat back in his chair, clasped his hands behind his head and said: "That was really good. Where did you buy it? I'll have to get some."

"I made it. From scratch," replied Mari eyeing him while tipping her wine glass upwards to drain the last few drops into her mouth.

"Is there pudding?" asked Johnny, a little abruptly.

"Not really," said Mari, whose confidence quickly faltered. "I thought the wine was enough extra calories. There are yoghurts in the fridge."

"Nah," said Johnny with a grimace. "I suppose you're right, I'll fill up on kebab or pizza later."

That felt like a kick in the stomach to Mari, who had lovingly prepared a fresh Italian recipe for him, which would later end up in a disgusting digestive stew in his stomach with takeaways and Jaegerbombs.

"Well, I'll have to love you and leave you," he said and stood up.

"Already?"

He walked round to Mari's side of the table, took her hand to encourage her to stand up, pulled her close and whispered: "It's a shame there's no time for *extras*. I'm well horny."

"Well, you should be staying," said Mari rather sternly.

He kissed her lips and made fake choking noises. "Garlic," he whispered, then bent over laughing.

Johnny always managed to tinge the evening with insult. Mari never felt good enough. She certainly didn't feel adored, which is what she always longed for.

"Have fun with your little boyfriends then," she said with a dollop of sarcasm. "And don't call me at 3am because I won't answer."

He was out in the stairwell when Mari remembered and shouted from her front door: "Oh – I almost forgot. My mum has invited us both to lunch on Sunday."

There was a long pause. Johnny winced, away from Mari's vision, and turned round to say: "Really? Do you think it's a good idea?"

"Yes. Why not?" she replied.

"Well then, if you want me to, I will. I didn't know we were at the 'meet the parents' stage."

"Neither did I," she agreed, stuck for anything else to say. "Pick me up at 11.30 then."

She shut the door. The dress got immediately dumped in the laundry basket, her hair was thrown up in a pony tail and she settled into her fluffy pyjamas in front of the telly with a bag of Maltesers.

"Screw the calories," she muttered. "If that wanker's going for it tonight, so am I."

CHAPTER FIVE

Nancy poured prosecco into bowl of freshly cut strawberries, humming along to Ella Fitzgerald and wiggling her hips.

"Waste not want not," she whispered then giggled and poured herself a glass of the bubbly. Bills footsteps echoed on the wooden floorboards in the hall leading to the kitchen.

"Oh shit," she said with the glass to her lips and half a mouthful of booze.

"Nance, it's 10am," Bill groaned.

"I know, I know! It's for the pudding really," she admitted, then burst out laughing. "Ah, who cares? Want one?"

"Go on then," said Bill smiling at his wife. "I don't have to drive anywhere today".

He sat at the breakfast bar and watched Nancy separate egg whites and yolks into separate bowls. He thought she was rather beautiful. Her chin-length brown hair –artificially coloured these days - always looked windswept and sophisticated and she rarely went a day without a touch of rose pink lipstick, even at work as a classroom assistant. Nancy was equally adoring of her husband with his head of peppery, silver hair and his face full of wisdom lines. He looked after himself and sported only a slight belly – not bad for fifty-eight. His main source of exercise was a regular round of golf with his work mates from the whisky distillery, overlooking the ocean at Lossiemouth's beach-side course, occasionally followed by a few drams and a begging call to Nancy to taxi him the six miles to home.

"What you making?" he enquired.

"Pavlova with prosecco-soaked strawbs and whipped cream." She raised her eyebrows with a naughty charm. "Maybe I'll eat some off you later!"

Bill guffawed and took a sip from his champagne flute. They both knew it would never happen, but they loved to flirt.

The kitchen was bright, with cream-painted wooden cupboards and imitation granite work tops. They had hoped to renovate the room, "the heart of the home," as Nancy referred to it, but having started saving for their youngest daughter's wedding that plan had been shelved.

The house, a detached bungalow surrounded by a neat garden and driveway, was in Elgin, a large town twenty-five miles or so east of Inverness. It had three bedrooms and a recently decorated living room was the pride and joy of the couple. They saw it as their reward for years of hard work and child-rearing. This was supposed to be their time to relax.

"I've been thinking, Bill," said Nancy tentatively, "maybe, since the wedding has been called off, we could go on holiday after all. Maybe get some sun in Italy or visit the south of France."

Bill tapped his glass thoughtfully. "Yes, I think we should." He lowered his voice for the next part of the sentence: "I'll have to find the right time to ask about getting the wedding money back," he looked over his shoulder, "but you leave that to me, love. We'll get ourselves a holiday."

"Eeeeh," squeaked Nancy. The prosecco was already going to her head.

"I'm really looking forward to lunch with the girls today," she said with a fond smile. "I know they don't always get on, but I think at a time like this, when one of them is suffering, it's important to bring them together and be a family."

She suddenly grew serious and stared wide-eyed at Bill. "I hope me asking Mari's man to join us won't upset Louisa. You know, if it feels like we're rubbing her sister's happiness in her face."

"No, sweet. You're over-thinking it," Bill said with a reassuring glance.

"Besides, she's twenty-nine, Nance. Twenty-bloody-nine. I worry about her. If she had been more independent then this break-up wouldn't have floored her as much. If she had a career and could afford to get her own place and stand on her own two feet, things would be so much better. I just don't know what we're going to do with her, you know, as we get older." Nancy placed her hand on her husband's. "I'm sure she'll be fine," she said softly. "Maybe this'll be the life event that jolts her into action and forces her to take more responsibility for herself. And if not, she can live with us until we are really old and it becomes her job to wipe our arses!" Nancy let out a cheeky chortle.

"Oh god, that's a terrifying thought," said Bill, holding his stomach and laughing a bit too loudly. "She'd be useless, we'd just be covered in it. And on that thought, I'm going to sort out the recycling."

He kissed his wife's cheek and left the room.

Nancy finished her enormous meringue mound and placed it in the oven, happily humming all the while.

CHAPTER SIX

Mari was zipping up her coat when Johnny texted to say he was outside in the car.

He had an eight-year-old Volkswagen Golf which he threw his spare cash at like it was his mistress. Blackened alloy wheels made it look "more sick", he had tried to convince Mari. She couldn't care less.

She ran down the stairs, clutching a bunch of pink roses, out the heavy main door, pausing to give it a light shove to ensure the lock clicked - there had been problems which the housing developers were taking their time to correct - and practically bounced into the car's passenger seat.

"Nice flowers," Johnny commented.
"They're for mum, they're her favourite," she replied fondly.

The forty-minute drive along the A96 was pleasant, albeit a bit loud for Mari, with Ministry of Sound blaring from the stereo.

They pulled up outside the house and Johnny gave a nervous sigh.

"You'll be fine," said Mari reassuringly. "Just to warn you, mum's a bit doo-lally and Louisa is… an attention-seeking drama queen. Dad is fine. He's easy."

They made their way up the short crazy-paved driveway to the front door, where Mari shoved the roses in Johnny's hand. Before he had a chance to ask, she explained: "You can't come here empty-handed, mum will never forgive you."

She rang the bell then opened the front door and walked in.

"Darling!" her mother cried with arms outstretched, muttering apologies about the floral apron she was wearing with sauce stains. "This must be Johnny," she enthused as though speaking to someone from a foreign land with little grasp on English. "How do you do?"

He smirked and shook her hand, but Nancy dove in for a hug and kissed his cheek. "I don't shake hands with family!"

He looked terrified.

"Bill," Nancy called out. "BILL!"

Bill came trotting through like a dog to his master and offered Johnny a firm hand to shake.

"Welcome," he said.

"Thanks," stuttered Johnny.

Mari used over the top eye signals to hint at the flowers.

"Oh, these are for you," said Johnny shyly handing them to Nancy.

"Wow, pink roses, my favourite," Nancy exclaimed with an air of suspicion and couldn't help but meet eyes with Mari.

"Let's go through to the lounge," declared Nancy. They never used to call it a lounge, that had only begun after the revamp. Firm, ivory-coloured settees lined two sides of the room and a large faux-marble fireplace took over one whole half of the room, or so it felt.

"Where's Louisa?" Mari asked.

"Oh, she'll be through soon," replied Nancy in hushed tones. "She's not really taking things well. She's spent most of her time in her room, well, the spare room," then turning to Johnny she commented: "We had it re-wallpapered last year, it's lovely."

He nodded with pretend interest, which Mari noticed and scored him mental points.

They sat in silence for a moment.

"I think once she meets up with some friends and maybe gets a little job she'll start to be like herself again," said Nancy with an assured smile.

"Hi," came a meek voice at the living room door. It was Louisa. She looked pale and tired, but still stunningly beautiful with her hair piled on top of her head in a messy bun. She wore a pair of tight jeans and a simply navy woolen jumper. Mari envied how her sister could look so good in something so simple, while it had taken her a few hours to pull together her own look: black leggings with a long black and grey striped top with her hair straightened numerous times over to make it silky. *That's what people do, right?* Mari had thought, when deciding what to do with her locks.

"How are you?" asked Mari gently.

"Fine," Louisa replied with a sweet smile.

"This is Johnny."

Johnny stood up and reached over to shake Louisa's delicate hand.

"Nice to meet you," said Louisa and sat down next to him on the sofa.

Mari gave an inward grunt. She would have to perch next to him, wouldn't she? She could already see Johnny going gooey over Louisa, it's just what men did.

Bill, who had been sitting silently in his chair in the corner finally spoke up: "Well, this is nice. It's been a while since we've had so many folk in this room, and to have a new addition as well, that's just great."

Nancy grinned at him and patted her knees decidedly before announcing: "Let's go and get this show on the road."

The all took their seats at the large dining table in the open plan kitchen and Nancy set about pouring wine for herself, Bill, Mari and Louisa and offered Johnny a cola.

She pressed play on the small CD player next to the microwave and instrumental exotic music began.

Mari and Louisa glanced at each other and burst out laughing.

"What *is* this?" Mari enquired through giggles.

"It's Yiddish music," said Nancy with a straight face, almost insulted. "Jewish."

"Are we having Jewish food?" asked Louisa with genuine interest now.

"No," said Nancy, sensing mockery.

Laughter rippled round the dining table until even Nancy saw the funny side.

"No good? Fine, I'll put on something more… acceptable to you straight-laced types."

"Your mother's got wanderlust again," explained Bill. "She's taken to this CD lately, and the Moroccan one. Oh, and Indian music." He placed his hand upon his brow and laughed, then turned to Johnny and whispered: "It's never dull with these women. Well, actually you'll be alright, Mari's probably the sane one."

With Jools Holland's rhythm and blues selected as their background music instead, Nancy began dishing out steaming mounds of white rice and chicken in white wine sauce. It was exquisite, her signature dish. Her daughters had eaten this on many occasion but never tired of it.

Halfway through the first course Bill turned to Johnny and asked: "Are you a whisky man?"

"Not really," was his response, which was met with a disappointed "Oh," from Bill.

"You're dad's in the furniture business isn't he?"

"Um, yes," said Johnny, suddenly sitting up like a school boy being asked for answers. "He's done that all his life. Expects me to do the same."

"And do you think you will?" asked Bill.

"Bill! Don't put the lad on the spot," interjected Nancy.

"It's OK," said Johnny comfortably. "I don't really know. I might stay on in the company, or I might go back to Greece."

This was news to Mari, who accidentally banged her fork off her plate and swallowed too quickly, forcing her to glug some wine.

Nancy and Bill exchanged surprised glances.

"Anyway, Mari, have you seen Louisa's eyelashes?" asked Nancy.

Louisa shifted uncomfortably in her seat. Mari noticed Louisa had gobbled her food quickly, but not touched her wine and was sipping glass after glass of water.

"What's different about them?" she asked politely, "Are they fake?"

"They're amazing," Nancy oozed.

"They're semi-permanent," Louisa explained. "They get glued on to your real lashes and last until those fall out in the natural renewal process. It's cool because you don't need to apply mascara or false lashes every day. I couldn't be without them," then she trailed off with a sudden realisation that life, for her, had changed beyond recognition and maybe stick on lashes were going to be a thing of the past.

"I think we should get some," said Nancy grinning and looking at Mari. "I could see if the beautician on South Street can do them."

"Maybe," Mari replied.

The phone rang in the hallway and Bill slowly rose from his seat.

"Leave it Bill," nagged Nancy. "We're with the girls. And Jonathan."

"Johnny," Johnny corrected her.

Regardless, Bill made his way out into the hall, closing the kitchen door behind him.

Five minutes passed, while Nancy downed her second glass of wine, and said with a giggle: "I'm getting a little tipsy. It's just fabulous."

The girls grinned and Louisa perked up and mouthed to Mari: "A little?"

Bill finally returned, looking a little shaken. They all looked at him, expecting bad news. When he failed to speak they glanced at each other in bewilderment.

"What is it darling?" Nancy enquired.

"That was…" he trailed off, unsure of whether or not to continue. "That was Justin. I don't know what time of day or night it is in Dubai but he sounded like he'd had a few drinks."

Louisa looked as though she might pass out or vomit. Her cheeks burned red and her eyes grew wide.

"He told me everything." Bill suddenly directed his stare at Louisa, boring into her soul. "He told me about the caretaker. And about the money."

Louisa began sobbing.

"Bill! Not now!" shrieked Nancy. "Whatever this is about, can wait till after lunch. We have *company* and there's still pavlova."

"No, Nance," he responded, raising his hand as if directing a "stop" signal. "I'm sick of being lied to and having to continually pick up the pieces."

"Dad!" cried Louisa. "It's not as bad as you think. Let me talk to you about everything later."

Bill turned on his heel and left the room, looking at the floor the whole time.

Louisa rushed out the door too, humiliated and hell bent on constructing some damage repair to her father-daughter bond.

"WHAT ABOUT THE PAVLOVA?" Nancy bellowed, which startled Mari and Johnny.

It was the first time Mari had felt like Johnny was actually on her team. They sat side by side in silence.

Brandishing a huge serving spoon, Nancy pointed it at Johnny and asked, seeming to be on the verge of hysteria: "Pavlova?"

CHAPTER SEVEN

Bill paced the garden for half an hour, head lowered, as if sailing through a fog of anger.

Nancy couldn't help but recite the rhyme "round and round the garden, like a teddy bear…" as she watched from the kitchen window. That had been her daughters' favourite bedtime ritual. Nancy used to draw circles on the girls' palms before delivering energetic tickles at the end of the rhyme. She could still hear her children's unbridled giggles in her mind.

Pans soaked in hot, soapy water in the sink below the kitchen window, as the dishwasher whirred into action. Nancy spooned yet more prosecco-berry pavlova into her mouth, straight from the serving plate, as she continued to gaze into the garden. She had a tendency to eat her way through stress.

The mound of crumbling meringue and berries was half-finished already, thanks to Mari and Johnny. They had lost their appetite immediately after the table-side drama, but had sensed that force-feeding themselves dessert was the right thing to do as they sat at the table, just the two of them and Nancy, in her lonely spot at one end of the table. It was awkward, but quick. Mari ate at speed, mumbling about how tasty it was, then kissed her mother, grabbed their coats and said she'd call the next day.

Louisa monitored Bill's slow circuits of the lawn from her bedroom window upstairs, her heart pounding like the beat of a repetitive dance track all the while.

She hadn't unpacked her huge Louis Vuitton suitcase. She was struggling to accept this was to be home for the time being. It stung, having to move back into her former childhood bedroom, at almost 30. What made it worse was that it had been decorated for its new use as the "guest room". The coffee-coloured floral wallpaper was practically shouting in her face that she should not be back here. The room had moved on and so should she.

Louisa's heart fluttered as Bill swerved off-course and headed for the back door and into the house. She listened, tracking his movements downstairs. The living room door was closed gently, Louisa observed, which was a good sign. Had it been slammed she probably wouldn't have made her next move, which was to tiptoe down the stairs and peer through the glass door panels into the room. Action burst onto the TV screen and she could see Bill's hand on the remote, skipping channels, as he lifted his feet wearily onto the footstool.

Louisa cautiously opened the door and looked meekly at her father, as if waiting for an invitation.

Bill examined her face and recognised the expression from every childhood telling off he had given her. His daughter's large blue eyes had always weakened him in these crucial moments of a stand-off.

He adored her, yet he knew the time had come for her to grow up.

"Can I come in?" asked Louisa softly.

Bill said nothing, but held his hand out as if summoning her to sit next to him.

She stepped over to the chair then suddenly dropped down and threw her arms over his body, wrapping her wrists around his neck and sobbed. "I'm sorry dad, I can explain everything. I never meant to lie."

She felt as if she were five years old, needing that feeling of safety she could only get in the arms of her father.

"Well," said Bill in a steady, cold voice, not wanting to show signs of softening, "you'd better get explaining."

Louisa launched an emotional monologue about her loneliness in Dubai, with a fiancé who was often away on business. When he was at home he had "social commitments" to drink in lavish nightclubs with his bosses or play sports to prove his drive and strength in the battle for Alpha male position in the group of men with promotion potential. She felt all he wanted was a girl on his arm at corporate events and she had begun to fear what she was signing up for: a loveless marriage to a business-obsessed stranger. She had made friends with many of the wives and fiancées of Justin's colleagues but never quite fitted in, she felt. It was competitive. They fought to have the priciest handbag collection, the most extravagant wedding plans and unusual hen parties. "Once, Kanye West turned up at a hen night!" Louisa explained in dramatic tones. Her father cared not for this and simply eyeballed her to get on with it.

It was all way out of Louisa's league and she was merely treading water in this social pool. The only saving grace was that she was picking up sewing skills quickly and had been promised a small part-time job by Mazzy, the couture dressmaker, who had been impressed with Louisa's enthusiasm. In truth, helping Mazzy with wedding dresses was the only thing that made Louisa feel worthy in the whirlwind of constant socialising with ladies of leisure. Obviously, the job had vanished in the same puff of smoke as her engagement and life of luxury.

The money went missing when it was her turn to treat The Wives, as their clique was termed, to an afternoon of cocktails and spa treatments. She had been on several of these indulgent sessions at the expense of other women's husbands, and she feared the bill was circling ever closer to her until one day the text message arrived. It was her turn to think up some fun. Money was never mentioned, because no-one gave it a second thought, apart from Louisa. Justin assured her he would set up a bank account for her after the wedding, but until then he would hand her a wad of notes on his way out the door. Louisa was too ashamed to keep asking for more to keep up with The Wives, so, often she would feign illness to avoid parties and lunches. But the time had come for her to pay-up or risk losing her only so-called friends. Bill interrupted the monologue at this point to predict what was coming.

"So you used MY money to get some rich bitches massaged?" he hissed, failing to completely bury his anger.

There was a pause, while Louisa searched for an alternative explanation, but failed to find one.

"Yes," she admitted. "The money you sent me to add to our wedding fund was still in my personal account. I swear I was going to replace it bit by bit whenever Justin gave me spending money, but of course I never got any more. I didn't expect to be chucked out before I could replace it."

"How could you be so stupid, Louisa?" her dad asked, through stiffened lips. "That was £5000 of mine and your mum's hard-earned cash. Do you know we sacrificed a holiday for that?"

She looked horrified and shook her head.

"We had the south of France booked. We lost a £200 deposit on that, just so we could give you a bit of money and claw back some dignity for us. Do you know how humiliating it is when your daughter's fiancé regards the amount you earn as pocket money? We knew 5000 would probably only buy one designer shoe for you, but it was all we could raise."

"Hardly," remarked Louisa, but she felt sick with shame.

"So…. is it *all* gone?" Bill asked with his eyes closed, fearing the answer.

"Yes." Louisa stared at Bill's jumper, afraid to make eye contact. "That's why I needed the money to fly home."

"Another few hundred," Bill groaned with a sigh.

An idea came to Louisa and she slipped off the diamond engagement ring she was still wearing on her right hand.

"Take this," she said shyly, "and sell it."

Bill glanced at the ring, then at his daughter's huge blue eyes and clasped his large, warm hand around the ring and her fingers with tears gathering in his eyes.

Without a word, he placed the ring in his pocket and nodded discreetly.

Louisa rested her head on her father's chest with a feeling or relief washing over her.

"You've missed a bit of your story," said Bill sternly.

Shit, this wasn't over yet.

"The caretaker?" Bill queried, with a cautious voice than indicated he wasn't sure he really wanted to know everything.

Louisa decided to heavily edit the details to protect her father. She would never tell him of the intense passion she felt for the young Thai man, who had devoured her like no man ever before.

46

Chati first encountered her on a swelteringly hot day. She was lying on the sofa in her apartment with a fan directed at her body, reading a novel and hiding from the rich wives. She wore nothing but a black bra and tiny purple knickers. Nudity had never bothered her, a fact which often caused arguments between her and Mari over the years. In their teens, Louisa would barge into Mari's room unannounced causing Mari to have a fit, screeching some paranoid rants about her body. "Get over yourself," Louisa would say. "I'm hardly here taking photos of you for Playboy!"

To Louisa, bodies were just flesh. Everyone had one, but then she'd never had cause to feel self-conscious, she was naturally slender, always had been. She was blessed, in the body department. Mari, on the other hand had always struggled with her weight. Her size fluctuated constantly. At her biggest, she had been a size 20, her smallest a size 12. She worked tirelessly to maintain her current healthy size.

On this hot day in Dubai, Chati was servicing air conditioning units in the apartment building. He had come straight to Dubai from a prestigious technical college in Thailand and fell into his handyman job by accident. He knew he could find better, but was happy to be earning until the right thing came along. He knocked on the door of Louisa's apartment, to which she replied with a hint of frustration: "Come in!"

47

Louisa assumed it would be Mazzy from a few doors down, who had been texting and calling her all morning trying to get her to join the gang for lunch.

Chati's eyes fell upon this stunning woman, draped across the settee.

"Oh, I'm so sorry ma'am," he exclaimed in a panic.

Louisa simply laughed and pulled a cushion in front of her, only partially hiding her body.

"No, I'm sorry," she said, still giggling. "I thought you were someone else. I should really be careful."

"I'm here to service the air conditioning," Chati explained, looking everywhere but at Louisa. "I can come back."

His voice was gentle and Louisa thought his south-east Asian accent was cute. She told him to go-ahead and assured him she would put on her robe.

For the 20 minutes Chati tinkered with the machine in the wall, the pair of them continuously stole subtle glances at one another. Chati's heart was pounding, while Louisa felt butterflies in her stomach. He finished the job, picked up his tool kit and bid Louisa good day. She walked with him to the door, her silk robe billowing in the breeze of the fan, revealing her smooth thigh. She thanked him with a huge grin and closed the door. She rested her back against the door for a few minutes smiling and wondering why on earth she was so excited, when all that had happened was the maintenance guy had done a quick job.

For the next two months, Chati and Louisa eyed each other in the hallway in passing, and Louisa would watch him accepting deliveries on the ground floor in the hot sun. She saw him interacting with a neighbour's child one afternoon in the hallway and knew from that moment he was a trustworthy soul.

One afternoon, alone again, Louisa felt the urge to draw Chati near. She didn't know his name by this point, or anything else about him for that matter. All she knew was that he was the most beautiful man she had ever seen and when their eyes met she felt nervous and euphoric at the same time.

She lay on her settee reading, as had become the habit, and jumped to her feet to peer through the door's spy hole into the stairwell every time she heard a noise. Neighbours came and went, but then in the middle of the afternoon on her fourth spy mission to the door, Louisa spotted her target. He was kneeling at his tool kit several feet away from her door. She opened it slowly, then after checking he was alone, dropped her silk robe to the ground, turned and walked back into the living room, throwing an inviting look his way, through the open door. Chati nervously considered the situation for a moment, then followed his instinct, and his raging desire, and entered the apartment.

What followed was the most intense meeting of flesh Louisa had ever experienced. She licked his skin and he grasped her body. They knew exactly what to do with each other, as if they had been in that moment before.

In the three months Chati was in Louisa's life, they only got intimate four times. The rest of their encounters were mere passing glances, but they thought of each other endlessly. They hardly knew a thing about one another, but the thing that Louisa would never forget was that Chati's name meant "life". She felt this was a fitting name, because she never felt more alive than when they were entwined.

And now here she was, sitting in her parent's house in Scotland being asked to sum up this longing in a few sentences. It was impossible. She couldn't explain to her father that this brief fling had blown everything she thought she knew about love out of the water. She couldn't tell him she felt a dull ache inside when she replayed that first passionate encounter again and again at night in bed, allowing tears to soak her pillow. He would never understand how two people could know so little about each other, yet feel the entire essence of their beings.

She searched for appropriate words to her dad's question and settled upon the mediocre sentence: "I was lonely and he made me happy. He was nice."

Those words felt like a betrayal of her real feelings, which were so intense she felt she finally understood Beyonce's song Crazy in Love. She felt insane. She couldn't control her desire.

"And how did Justin find out about you and... him?" asked her dad, stroking her arm protectively.

"Dad. There are some things you don't need to know," she responded, hoping this would halt the interrogation. Louisa could not face telling her father that Justin had found used condoms in the bathroom bin whilst rummaging for his old razor head, after realising he'd run out. There were some things they need never tell each other.

"You're right, sweetheart," her dad agreed, slightly embarrassed.

Then, after a moment of deep thought he added: "I suppose I find it hard to understand because I was sitting here on my little sofa feeling proud that my girl had finally landed on her feet, with a man who could look after her and provide for her, in a way I never could for your mum."

"But he didn't look after me," Louisa protested. "Yes, he threw money at me now and then, but he wasn't there for me. He didn't love me." She was on the verge of tears. "Not the way that you love mum."

They hugged silently for a few minutes, until Bill spoke up once more.

"So, what are you going to do with yourself? You know you can't stay here forever at your age. You'll need a job."

Louisa felt hurt, that their moment of tenderness had been shattered by thoughts of practicality.

"I know that," she responded defensively. "I'll sort things out. I'll start job hunting in the morning."

"What about that phlebotomy course we put you through a few years ago? Can't you use that to get a job taking blood at the hospital?" he asked.

Louisa couldn't admit that there was nothing to show for the £300 he and Nancy had spent on the course. If students who passed the two-day course failed to use the skills they gained on rubber veins within 18 months on real people with real blood their certificates were no longer valid. Hers had long been invalid.

"Maybe," she replied shiftily. "Leave it to me."

With that she rose and went towards the door.

Nancy, who'd been listening at the door with tears in her eyes, jumped and hot-footed back to the kitchen, undetected.

Upstairs, Louisa lay on her temporary bed feeling exhausted and traumatised after the heart-to-heart. She looked at her bare hands, where, until that day, a diamond had sparkled, acting as a reminder that she had once been happy with a future plan. Now the slate really was wiped clean.

She lay down and tried not to think of Chati, which was impossible. She'd been attempting to bury her memories of him deep inside, but it felt as though while she spoke with her dad she was metaphorically grave-digging – thrusting her spade into the fresh mound of emotional soil thrown over her and Chati.

CHAPTER EIGHT

A little more red here, thought Mari clicking on a text box on screen. She was creating a poster for the shop window about a 20% off sale weekend. Pictures of plump sofas and temptingly puffed up bedding were surrounded by bold text. "It needs to be more… in your face," Steve had barked over her shoulder moments before.

She could hear muffled female giggling through the wall. "Hee hee hee," mocked Mari in a bitter high-pitched voice, screwing up her face. "I'm so pretty and if you buy all these hideous lamps I'll sit on your face."

Johnny was in the office next door with a lighting sales rep. They had been in there for 36 minutes. Suddenly the door to the office opened and Johnny popped his head round and into the doorway of her small office and said chirpily: "Mar, can you grab us a couple of cappuccinos from the machine?"

He winked and returned to his meeting, shutting the door abruptly.

"Cheeky bastard," Mari muttered quietly and set about making the coffees.

She'd never felt this possessive of a man before, but somewhere in her desperation to settle down and create a family she had rolled all her hopes and her feelings into a mess, like the hairdryer, straighteners and phone charger cables next to her bedside table at home. It was too difficult to see clearly which cable

belonged to which appliance, and Mari
was similarly finding it increasingly difficult to identify
which feelings belonged to reality and which were mere
fantasy.

She had reached a point where he either had to
become her full-blown boyfriend and spend more time
with her - and not just eating her food - or something
was going to have to change. It was this alternative
option that scared her. In the still of night, she
occasionally saw things with clarity, as if viewing her
life from a distance, and knew the relationship wasn't
working. She couldn't see Johnny as a father, he was
still in child-mode himself.

Fear came stomping into her thoughts to warn
her that there might never be another man, especially
not one so good-looking. Despite his lack of
commitment, or respect, he did make her feel desirable
at times and she got swept up in his fun-seeking
spontaneous attitude, which was good for someone like
her, who rarely stepped out her comfort zone willingly.

Mari convinced herself that if they dated long
enough, Johnny could maybe learn to build his life
around hers and would magically fall deeply in love
and want children. She already had a wedding dress
inside a black dress bag at the back of her wardrobe, her
darkest secret yet. It was £50, on sale from £200,
recently and she justified the purchase as future
investment. She fantasised about wearing the gown at
Inverness registry office with Johnny. Even her dreams

were low key - she didn't feel she deserved to dream of a country mansion wedding. She felt she'd be lucky enough if she lured a man to the altar at all, so a bland local authority altar would suffice.

Lunchtime came, and still Johnny's voice boomed through the wall, to replies of flirtatious feminine giggles. Mari drowned this out by calling her mum, as promised.

"So, what happened yesterday?" Mari enquired with a long slow breath, preparing herself for drama.

"Oh, you know," said Nancy timidly.

"No, I don't," Mari replied.

"Well, I haven't pried, but from what I gather, Louisa was having an affair and that's why Justin threw her out." She quickly added in a panicked voice: "Don't tell her I told you. Let her tell you when she's ready."

"I won't," she said sincerely. "But, that explains it. I have to say, I'm not surprised."

"Mari!" scolded Nancy. "It sounds like she was having a tough time."

Not according to her Facebook page, thought Mari, who had enviously clicked 'like' to numerous photographs over the past six months of Louisa and fellow socialites sunning themselves and drinking mojitos.

"What was the thing about the money?" Mari asked, more interested in this part, having seen her parents bail Louisa out of financial difficulties far too many times.

"Well, I'm not sure if I should say…." Nancy said with hesitation. "They've sorted it out now anyway. Your dad is getting some of it back."

"I knew it! I knew it would involve you and dad!" Mari spluttered. "How much?"

"Mari, that's *her* business," Nancy insisted. "It's getting sorted out, OK. Anyway," she continued, desperate to change the subject, "it was nice meeting Jonathan yesterday."

"It's Johnny, not Jonathan," she replied with a smile. "What did you think of him?"

There was a pause before Nancy replied with restraint: "He's a nice guy."

"Yes… is that it?" Mari was disappointed. She wanted her mum's seal of approval, or at least words of reassurance from someone else that their paring wasn't ridiculous.

"He seems a bit young in his ways, a little bit immature, compared to you, but then I didn't really get to know him properly. I could be wrong. He's very handsome," she added, quickly steering the conversation to more positive waters.

"Too handsome for me?" Mari asked desperately.

"Don't be daft!" her mother bellowed. "You're gorgeous. And classy. He's a lucky man."

Mari felt a warm glow of happiness from the praise.

"Listen," said Nancy, interrupting the pleasure. "There's something I need to ask you."

"Uh huh?" replied Mari suspiciously.

"I overheard your dad telling Louisa it's time she stood on her own two feet and I think she's going to be looking for a job and a place to stay, away from us…"

Mari knew what was coming.

"No, she can't move in with me!"she quickly cried, before the question came. "We'd end up bickering and getting up each other's noses. Plus, Johnny might be moving in with me," she lied for extra excuses. She hadn't noticed Johnny and the lighting rep were saying their goodbyes at the doorway and as he walked past he nervously caught Mari's eye. Her heart raced, unsure of whether or not he had heard what she foolishly said.

"Really?" said Nancy with a hint of sarcasm. She knew Mari was bluffing. "I had no idea you were at that stage."

"Well, we might be soon," she replied in slight hushed tones, in case he was still within earshot.

"All I'm asking is that you think about it, and it wouldn't be forever," said Nancy with certainty, as if the decision had already been made. "It would make me very happy to know my girls are both safe. I don't like you living alone and god forbid Louisa gets into some awful bedsit, she wouldn't survive. She's never been good at organising her life, like you are, dear. Besides, she might not even ask you, I'm just giving you a heads up."

They signed off affectionately and Mari agreed to consider it, although she would rather shack up with the devil than share a roof with her sister.

A lifetime of walking in the shadows of her younger sister had filled her with a bitter resentment. At every monumental life moment of Mari's it felt as though Louisa was plotting to steal her thunder. Mari passed her cycling proficiency test as school, so Louisa fell off her bike and had to get stitches, which took up the whole afternoon and meant the family forgot to celebrate. When Mari passed her exams and got into university Louisa ran away for four days for some telling off she'd had about skipping school. Bill and Nancy almost missed Mari's graduation because Louisa was in hospital overnight to have her stomach pumped, probably after another one of her college binge drinking sessions. Her parents made it to the ceremony just in time, but Mari never forgot that empty seat next to them in the auditorium.

Sunday's meal was yet another example of Louisa ruining a big moment for her older sister. Fair enough, she hadn't chosen the timing for her distraught ex-fiancé to call, but still, her actions had completely engulfed Mari's first family meal with her boyfriend in chaos and negativity.

The idea of her peaceful home life being shattered by emotional uproar was less than appealing.

Johnny returned from waving off the rep and entered Mari's office as she bit into a sandwich.

"Shall I come over to see you after dinner?" he asked, with a smirk, which put Mari off her food. Either he was pretending he hadn't heard her revelation that he was to be her live-in-lover, or the rep's squeaky voice had genuinely overpowered the phone conversation and she was safe.

"Why don't I come over to yours for a change?" asked Mari attempting puppy dog eyes. "We're always at mine, and it would be nice to go somewhere different."

Aside from the fact it was costing her a lot more in food to have Johnny round, she was getting paranoid that he never wanted to be seen out with her. Was he hiding her?

"Nah, it's boring at mine," said Johnny frowning. "You know I live with my parents. It sucks."

"I know that," said Mari "but it would be nice to be able to picture where you are when you're not with me."

He raised his eyebrows. Mari wondered if she was coming across as too clingy.

"Well, mum's making lasagne tonight," said Johnny, getting Mari's hopes up for an invitation, "so I have to go home for that, but I'm free after if you want me to come over. If not, I'll see you another night."

Mari's smile suddenly dropped and she couldn't hide her disappointment. "No, it's fine, come round."

Ten minutes later, Johnny texted while out on his lunch break at the Costa across the retail park. "Forgot I already said I'd do something tonight. Soz. Will catch you tomorrow night? x"

Mari examined the contents of this text for so long it brought her to tears. One kiss. Soz.

She just wanted to be adored.

Without thinking it through, Mari replied by text, saying: "If you hate it that much at your mum and dad's why don't you move into mine? xxx"

With the click of "send" she felt panic flush through her system. The words psycho and desperate sprung to mind.

Twenty seconds later, her panic was replaced with confusion and disappointment when he replied with a simple "ha ha." These emotions were quickly swept away by humiliation.

CHAPTER NINE

The cool water rippled and flowed around Mari's body as she swum the length of the pool. It was Wednesday night and the water was busy with bobbing heads, all there to the same end – to burn a few calories and tone up.

She liked to swim after work. It gave her a sense of relief after being cooped up in her little windowless office all day. That, and she felt it would help cancel out the scone and butter she had devoured at 4 o'clock that afternoon, or at least the butter anyway.

She was on breaststroke length number 10, motoring around in silence, apart from the pop songs floating around the pool side from the radio system.

She flipped onto her back to back crawl the rest of the length, looking up at the shiny wooden ceiling, aware that water was blocking all sound. It was bliss. It gave her thoughts room to manoeuvre.

It had been two days since the dreadful "move in with me" text and while she had seen Johnny at work, he hadn't been round to hers. Mari wondered if he was avoiding her. He was being polite at work and nothing more. No kisses, no cheeky bum slaps, like he had done regularly before. *Boyfriends aren't supposed to be on polite mode with their girlfriends*, Mari thought angrily. *I'm not his granny!*

She was gradually accepting that rather than bringing her happiness, this relationship was making her paranoid and needy. Mari had lived on her own for years, yet here she was acting as if her every ounce of joy depended on someone else. She would have to be brave and pull the rug from under this farce, she decided.

She would give the wedding dress to Oxfam and pretend that whole wardrobe secret never happened.

Suddenly, Mari's hand sunk into the furry flesh of an elderly man's back and she grabbed hold of the plastic lane divider to steady herself and turn around to apologise. Lost in her thoughts she had been drifting off course slightly and had launched her arm backwards into the next lane. "I'm so sorry," she gushed. "Dinnae worry hen," said the delighted soul, "I thought it was my lucky day!"

After swimming, Mari felt slim and energised... for all of 20 minutes, until she bought a bag of steaming hot chips on the way home.

She sat on the settee shovelling them into her mouth with her fingers, barely pausing for breath.

Next up was a glass of merlot and a browse through the TV channels to waste an hour or so before bed.

A single tear ran down her cheek, causing her to wipe it quickly with her sleeve and mutter "man up" to herself.

Picking up her phone, she wondered who to text. Most of her friends in Inverness were busy with wedding plans or raising children. She didn't want to hear about any of that at this moment.

Her closest friends from university lived hours away in Aberdeen, so she had hardly kept in touch lately. She realised how lonely she was.

"If you need somewhere to stay you can move in here, but you have to get a job and pay rent," she typed in a text to Louisa. She hesitated before sending the message and added a kiss at the end to soften it up.

Mari thought that perhaps a dance with the devil would be better than no dance at all.

CHAPTER TEN

Nancy and Louisa settled into their seats, unravelling their scarves and kicking their handbags under the table so they were out of sight. The coffee shop was packed with caffeine addicts, who had never really cared for the drink until this chain business popped up in Elgin five years before, but now it was all the rage. The town had caught up with trendy espresso-gluggers the world over, and youngsters from this part of the world finally knew their way around a venti skinny latte with hazelnut syrup.

Louisa placed the cappuccino in front of her mother and took the peppermint tea. They sliced a carrot cake and chocolate muffin, then swapped halves so they could try a bit of both. The pair were such bad decision makers, this was always the way out of cashier turmoil – sharing cakes.

Louisa placed her plastic bag on the empty seat beside her. Nancy had bought her daughter a plain black shirt for a job interview at an up-market restaurant on the banks of the River Ness, which flows through Inverness city centre. She was quite excited, having been wined and dined there by wealthy men twice before. It was the kind of establishment she could see herself working in, rather than a greasy bacon roll type of cafe. It had a spectacular view of the castle and attracted a trendy crowd.

Louisa's interview was in two days' time. First she had the small matter of getting her enormous suitcase through to Inverness.

"I'm a little bit nervous about moving in with Mari," said Louisa, picking up her fork eagerly.

"Well, that's understandable," said Nancy gently. "I know you two haven't always seen eye to eye, but I think it could be good for you both."

Louisa looked curiously at her mum.

"I know Mari's lonely," she said with concern. "I don't think this thing with Jonathan will last, I just have a feeling, and you need a place to live, so it's obviously good for you."

"But I always feel like she hates me," said Louisa between chews of cake.

"No, no, I think she gets jealous," revealed Nancy.

"What of?" asked Louisa with genuine surprise.

"Well, you've always been nice and slim and had lots of friends. She sees you out on adventures that she would never dream of."

"But I'm a fuck up, excuse my language," Louisa interjected. "I was sure she hated me because I continuously mess things up."

"Well..." Nancy paused to choose her words carefully. "I think when you have your ups and downs, it naturally draws our attention to you. You seem to have always been in the foreground and she seems to prefer it in the background. You took those opposing roles from early childhood. We should have never called her Mari."

"How so?" Louisa asked.

"I didn't find out until a few years ago when I tried to order Christmas presents with your name meanings on them that Mari means bitter!" Nancy let out a giggle. "I think that's what you call nom... nomin... nominative determinism."

"What's that?" asked her daughter.

"It's when someone called Mr Candle goes on to be a candle-maker and so on."

"Oh, I see," said Louisa then suddenly burst out laughing. "So you think you've made Mari bitter by giving her that name!"

"I'm not going to tell her it means bitter," Nancy said. "She won't find that funny. Your name means famous warrior."

They exchanged smiles of approval.

"I'd say you've got the famous bit down to a tee," Nancy continued, "with the glamour and all your shenanigans, but the warrior bit... we'll see about that one. Life throws events at you to test you – I think your warrior is still emerging."

Louisa smiled, glad to think there was at least one person who had faith in her. She sipped her tea thoughtfully for a moment then said. "I've always been jealous of Mari for knowing what she wants out of life and just getting on with it."

"See, maybe she needs to hear that," said Nancy. "Living together could be a chance to see each other in a new light."

"When did you become Oprah Wimphrey?" Louisa said with a laugh.

Diane Smith, whose daughter had been in Louisa's class at school, appeared behind Nancy with a tray of drinks. "Oh, hello!" she shouted. "Let me just put these to the table and come back!"

"Great," said Nancy quietly to Louisa with a hefty dose of sarcasm. Nancy had tried to like Diane when the girls were young, but coffee mornings had always revolved around whatever achievement had gone on in the Smith household. She was dull, and full of herself.

She waddled back and rubbed Louisa's shoulder.

"What are you doing home?" she bellowed. "How is life in the sun?"

Louisa blushed and said: "Oh, well, I'm back here now. Moving to Inverness tomorrow."

"Oh?"

Diane's expression was similar to that of a Parisian mime artist in utter disbelief - completely over the top. All she needed was the white facepaint and a stripy jumper and she would have been perfect.

"Yes, we're glad to have her back," said Nancy cutting in. "It was too far away."

"I suppose it is," replied Diane. "How are the wedding plans coming along?"

"They're not," said Louisa curtly, wanting to get this exchange over with as quickly as possible. "But who needs a man, right?" she added, trying to lighten the mood a little.

Diane's next act as a mime artist was to search for her lost puppy, looking all around her with worry and sadness in her eyes. Louisa began to smirk. "It's OK Diane," she said. "I'm moving on."

"Good, dear," then she turned to Nancy and spoke softly, only a few inches away from Nancy's nose. "It's not nice when your children's lives fall to pieces is it? It breaks your heart."

Nancy cleared her throat, feeling very uncomfortable with Diane's face so close to hers. "I'm not worried for Louisa," she insisted. "She'll be fine."

These words meant a lot to Louisa, even if they were just a cover-up for Diane.

"Oh, you're quite right," remarked Diane, suddenly changing her tone to happy mime artist. "I must go. We'll have to catch up soon so I can show you photos of Lilian's wedding. Her husband's a doctor. And they've a baby on the way. So exciting. Take care!"

Louisa and Nancy sighed with relief and smiled at one another.

"I bet the baby's as ugly as its grandmother," Nancy whispered, making Louisa choke on her tea.

They chatted about bargains and moisturisers for a while, and then Nancy found a way to steer the conversation in the direction she had been itching to go.

"Tell me, if you feel you can, about this other man," said Nancy cautiously, not wanting to upset her daughter.

Louisa was startled. She stroked the rim of her tall glass cup with her forefinger and said: "What do you want to know?"

"How did you meet? Was he handsome? Was he special?" There was a faint smile at the corner of Nancy's lips, which gave Louisa confidence to confide.

"He was absolutely stunning," she said, looking into her mum's eyes. "He did jobs around the apartment building and we would catch each other's eye. We never had much time together."

"He meant something to you didn't he?"

"How can you tell?" asked Louisa.

"You must have felt strongly for him to risk everything you had," said Nancy wisely. "And the way you spoke there said it all. He effected you."

Louisa's eyes filled with liquid until she could no longer see and had to dab them with a napkin to release the tears. Her mum held her hand.

"I've been there, darling. I know what it's like."

Louisa looked at her mum in confusion. "When?" she asked softly, sniffing.

"Before your dad," replied Nancy. "I've never told you this. Or Mari. In fact, I've hardly told anyone. I was working as a live-in nanny when I left school..."

"I knew about that," interrupted Louisa.

"... and when the husband, Greg was his name, broke his ankle and had to stay at home for three weeks we began to get to know each other. When the children went for afternoon naps, I would sit by him on the sofa and he would read me poetry in a velvety voice. He was so handsome with glossy black hair and a thick moustache – it was the seventies!"

Louisa was grinning, gobsmacked by the story that was unfolding.

Nancy took a sip then continued: "Anyway, eventually one thing led to another and we were making love regularly when the children napped. He was my first. I was head over heels. Then, out of the blue, his wife called to say I was no longer needed at the house. I think she found out."

"I can't believe this!" exclaimed Louisa. "I thought you were so innocent."

"I was, really," replied Nancy. "Well, naive, more than innocent. I phoned the house one afternoon, knowing he would be there alone, and all he said to me was 'never call this house again, you little fool'. I was heartbroken."

Nancy raised a mischievous eyebrow and said: "You're not the only one who meddles with danger, I tell you. Of course, ever since I met your dad I've been a good girl."

They laughed and Louisa felt the weight of her shame lift slightly, knowing even someone as whole and stable as her mother had made mistakes.

CHAPTER ELEVEN

Mari scribbled a few notes in a small pad beside her computer at work. She was trawling every job website she could find. Three items on the list had potential. The jobs were nothing special, but anywhere else would be a breath of fresh air compared to Williamsons and Sons Furniture.

Besides, Mari needed a quick getaway plan. She'd been gearing herself up to tackle issues head on and today was the day. It was Friday. She could throw the grenade and run off into the weekend.

If she could land another job soon it would mean only having to suffer a few weeks working among the wreckage of a failed relationship.

She hoped Johnny would take the break-up well. She couldn't predict his response - another sign he was not Mr Right, she barely knew the real Johnny.

Mari had on red lipstick and wore her best blouse - cream with a black collar - for confidence. If she was to believe in herself and say what she felt, she needed to feel proud to be Mari, not ashamed and wishing to hide.

An advert for an online dating website popped up to the right of the job search on screen.

Mari's gaze was diverted to the incredibly hot man smiling back at her from the ad. She clicked it, feeling like a naughty school girl. In her empowered mood, as she steam-rollered through her life choices, she thought she may as well have a quick look to see what was out there.

Just as she was about to fill in the registration details, which would allow her to roam the online candy store of eligible bachelors (she wouldn't let previous disappointments scar her dream of romance), Johnny tentatively entered the office.

She quickly hit the X at the corner of the page to close it down and turned to him with a straight face.

"Hi," he said nervously. "Sorry, I've not been texting, I've just been really busy."

"Yeah, it's not working out is it?" Mari blurted out without giving herself time to prepare a build-up speech. She had been dreading this moment all morning, so her natural reaction was to launch the plan without delay.

Johnny smiled with relief.

He's smiling, she thought in disbelief. Mari felt crushed. She had envisaged this moment to be emotionally charged with demands for her to explain herself. She had even hoped, perhaps too optimistically, for a little pleading.

"It's not," he agreed.

"Fine then," said Mari, fighting furiously to hold back tears.

"Fine," he replied, his smile slowly turning into worry at the sight of a woman on the verge of crying.

"We could still be friends with benefits," he suggested with a cautious grin.

Mari looked at the ceiling, then her hands, all the while the tears gathered in the corners of her eyes and her lips began to curl downward. *Shit, this is happening, I'm going to explode into crying*, she thought. *Don't do this Mari, hold it together.*

"I don't think that would be a good idea," she said, her voice breaking at the last word.

"I'll see you around," said Johnny with an apologetic smile.

"Yep," she replied, looking away from him before the floodgates opened.

The closest thing she had to a potential life mate turned and left the room and Mari was alone with the realisation that it was officially over.

CHAPTER TWELVE

Louisa and Bill lugged the huge suitcase up the one flight of stairs to Mari's front door, while Nancy trailed behind with a wicker basket full of food in the crook of one elbow and the carry handle of her old sewing machine in the hand opposite.

They were puffed out, but exchanged excited smiles as Louisa pressed the door bell.

A minute passed and Louisa shuffled from foot to foot impatiently then tried the bell again.

They heard some movement through the door, then a wailing sort of voice saying loudly: "I'm coming!"

Mari eventually turned the key, in agonisingly slow motion, pulled the security chain away and opened the door to a shocking sight. She was still in her pyjamas at lunchtime and her eyes were puffy and raw. She sniffed and wiped her nose on her sleeve, which made Nancy wince.

Mari extended her arms towards her mother with a cry of: "It's over with Johnny."

"There, there," soothed Nancy, stroking her daughter's back. "Let us in and we can sort you out. I really think you should have a nice shower."

Nancy shot a look of panic at Bill, who shrugged his shoulders dismissively.

"Ah, Mar," Bill said in a light-hearted way. "Better off without him, eh?"

Mari just sobbed and led the way to the small open plan living area. Louisa was left trailing behind with her suitcase.

"Sorry to hear that, sis," said Louisa affectionately. "Just as well I'm here now. We can be spinsters together."

"I don't want to be a spinster," wailed Mari with a fresh burst of self-pity.

Nancy spotted two empty crisp bags on the dining table, an empty bottle of wine and an open box of Celebrations. She gathered them up, binned the packets and placed the chocolates in the nearest cupboard.

"Go and get washed and dressed darling," she said encouragingly, "and I'll make us all a cup of tea, OK?"

Nancy set about boiling the kettle and emptying the contents of her basket onto the kitchen counter, as if creating a shop display: large items at the back, small items at the front, all in a slight semi-circle.

Bill picked up a small glass jar from the display and read aloud: "Tape – nade?"

"It's pronounced ta-pe-nad!" said Nancy with a smirk. "It's crushed olive paste."

"What the hell are they supposed to do with that?" he snorted.

"Eat it with these," said Nancy proudly tapping the box of bruschetta crisp breads.

Louisa raised her eyebrows and caught her dad's eye. They both tried not to laugh.

"Thanks mum, looks yum," she said. "I love that you always buy us strange things."

"Strange?" Nancy queried. "You mean interesting! There's a few packets of couscous and noodles there too, for basic meals."

Nancy felt a warm, maternal satisfaction when giving her girls food packages. It was one of the few things she could still do for them.

Mari emerged from her bedroom, clean, warm and wearing a pair of grey tracksuit bottoms and a black long-sleeved top. She looked more comfortable.

Her hair hung down below her shoulders, unstyled, but silky.

"That's better," declared Nancy. "We'll be in Spain from tomorrow so I'm glad I don't have to leave you on your own like this."

"Spain?" asked Mari, her eyes darting between her parents curiously.

"Yep," said Bill, barely able to contain his joy. "Two whole weeks. We'll phone you halfway through to see how you are. How you both are," he added turning towards Louisa. "It'll be good to get away together."

Bill and Nancy exchanged a loving smile.

"That's great," said Mari, still a little meek from her trauma. "You don't have to phone us, we're not kids. Just enjoy yourselves."

"Yeah, we'll be fine," added Louisa. "I'll make sure this one watches plenty of chick flicks and bitches about her ex to cleanse herself." She gives a nervous giggle, unsure of if she had overstepped the mark or not.

"I can watch Bridget Jones's Diary and see how much like her I am as I weep and belt out the song All By Myself," said Mari sarcastically.

Louisa rolled her eyes, out of everyone's view.

"Seriously though, that's a great idea," said Nancy to Mari, with a subtle warning. "Your sister's going to be here at exactly the right time. Just think, two gorgeous young women, starting afresh together. You can put the world to rights and go out on the pull together."

The girls both laughed.

"The pull?" said Mari, finally smiling. "You never know."

"Here, this will get your conversation flowing," said Bill producing a bottle of fine malt whisky from work.

Both Louisa and Mari hated whisky but thanked their dad politely.

After tea and biscuits, Nancy and Bill hugged their daughters and left, barely able to stop grinning with holiday anticipation.

Louisa and Mari sighed and smiled at each other.

"This is your room," said Mari, striding towards the spare bedroom. It was completely bare apart from cream curtains, a pine double bed and a pine chest of drawers.

Wow, that's bland, thought Louisa, popping her head into the room she would be calling home, for who knew how long.

"I'll grab my things and get settled in... if that's cool."

"Of course," said Mari. "Listen, I know it can't have been easy having to move back, and with all the stuff that's gone on..." she couldn't look at Louisa. "So, just... make yourself at home."

"Thanks," said Louisa, edging towards tears and lunged at Mari with a hug.

Mari was taken aback, but wrapped her arms around her sister. It felt familiar and strange at the same time. Since teenage years they had hardly spent a whole day together.

Louisa pulled her belongings into the room and pushed the door to within a centimetre of being closed – she felt it would be too rude to close the door at this stage.

She plugged in a small speaker to her phone and picked some music to unpack to. It was an electro swing mix of songs. Pumping beats and heavy basslines mixed with 1920s brass notes and samples of vintage singers in a style that Mari had never heard before. She was leafing through a magazine, sitting on the sofa. She sat forward, listening with interest. Mari walked towards Louisa's new room and paused at the door, before knocking and shyly popping her head in.

"What's this music?" she asked.

"It's electro swing," replied Louisa brightly.

"It's amazing," said Mari. "I've never heard anything like it."

"Oh my god, there's loads like this," said Louisa, grinning, "I can find heaps for you. I've got some CDs in the case too, of similar things.... Caro Emerald and such."

"Who?" asked Mari, feeling a bit exposed.

"You are going to LOVE her," Louisa said, getting a bit giddy with excitement. She had always displayed her emotions easily, a trait Mari envied.

Louisa rummaged in her case, which was a mess of tangled clothing and toiletries and produced a small pile of postcards and a pack of blu-tack.

She turned to Mari with uncertainty and asked: "Do you mind if I use blu-tack on the walls?"

"Of course not," said Mari. "Do anything you like. I've been thinking I need to decorate the whole place, I just couldn't decide on styles. You can paint it black if you like!"

They both laughed and Louisa said: "Well, I won't go that far, but thank you. I just can't settle in a place until it feels like mine."

Five minutes later there were black and white art cards stuck up in a vertical line above her bed, candles and a small, mirror jewellery box on the chest of drawers, a bright geometric-patterned cushion on the cream bed covers, adding a splash of much-needed colour, and a string of fabric birds in the middle of the window hanging from the curtain rail. Mari was gobsmacked.

"How have you managed to make this room look lived in when you've only been in it minutes?"

Louisa grinned and strutted across the floor to a song about girls in vintage clubs. She wiggled her hips and exclaimed in an old-style American theatrical accent: "darling, I just have the touch!"

This was the Louisa Mari remembered from childhood. Suddenly, she was hit with a surge of emotions. She felt joyful to suddenly realise there was still a dose of sisterly fondness in there she hadn't tapped into for years and guilty for ignoring it for so long. Her heart swelled to watch her sister strutting and singing, just as she had in her pink bedroom 20 years ago. They used to dance to the Spice Girls and Eternal in their rooms with pretend microphones. Life was so simple back then, and the sisters were so supportive of each other.

It struck Mari that, perhaps, they could rekindle this, or some of their former bond at least.

"Here's an idea," Mari suddenly blurted out. "Come with me to Homebase or B&Q or Asda or wherever and help me choose things for the rest of the flat. I want it to look like this," she said as she drew a circle in the air referring to the bedroom style.

"OK!" said Louisa eagerly. "Brilliant."

***

In just one night the flat was transformed. Mari and Louisa had devoted their Saturday evening to painting a feature wall 'dusky plum' in the living room area and adding splashes of purple and hot pink throughout the adjoining kitchen and dining area with cushions, place mats and mugs. It was a small room – used for everything – but at least now it had character.

A statement picture hung on the new plum wall – a large black and white printed butterfly in a chunky white wooden frame and purple glass candle holders sat where the framed selfie of Mari and Johnny had been. The happy picture had been haunting Mari for days, so she took great pleasure in dropping it into the industrial-sized wheelie bin outside the flats. She couldn't help but feel a pang of fear that there were no more images of that handsome face to pine over. He was removed from her home life in every way.

Louisa was conscious of allowing Mari to make the style decisions, however tempting it was to throw her own over-excited ideas in the pot. With Louisa being a bold risk-taker of a shopper, and Mari being the kind who likes to go home and mull over potential purchases before then returning to the shop three days later to find the items sold, they had made a pretty good team. Mari knew what she liked, she just needed a little shove from her sister to take the retail leap.

With what little money Louisa had, she bought a flat pack desk and chair that was reduced in Argos, which she had big plans for as her bedroom sewing station.

It was 2am, after a long painting and "sprucing" session, and Louisa whipped up whisky sour cocktails, using sugar, lemon juice and the whisky from their dad, to celebrate the decoration.

The sisters sat on the sofa opposite the new artwork, clinked glasses and both screwed up their faces at the first sip of booze.

"Urgh!" gasped Mari, before taking a second sip to examine the flavours. "It actually tastes better after the initial shock of tanginess."

Louisa laughed: "Maybe I haven't balanced the flavours quite right. I used to love these in this little cocktail bar near the water in Dubai. It wasn't quite as sharp as this!"

Louisa was feeling a little woozy. She couldn't tell if the paint fumes, exhaustion from the lack of sleep thanks to her thoughts keeping her awake most nights, or the rich tapenade on crackers the girls had scoffed instead of a meal between paintbrush strokes. The whisky wasn't sitting well in her stomach.

"I feel a bit sick," said Louisa suddenly. "I think I'm going to head off to bed soon."

"OK," said Mari. "Hope you're alright."

Just mentioning the word Dubai had given Louisa a tummy flip. She had barely thought about Justin, but when she did she felt a terrible, deep guilt. Although she was sure he didn't truly love her, she felt sorry for stamping all over the future he was trying to build for her. What hurt more than the guilt, however, was the feeling that Louisa would never lay eyes on Chati again. She imagined he would find someone else and carry on with his life in the sun, viewing Louisa as just a quick fling, or maybe even forget her.

Every night the tears kept flowing, surprising Louisa, who had begun to wonder if her eye sockets could be damaged by so much crying. She had Googled this at 3am one night in bed and been reassured by some answers about the cleansing properties of tears. *My tear ducts have had a bit of a colonic irrigation for the eyes*, thought Louisa in an attempt to make herself laugh.

She slipped into her new bed and smiled to discover a fluffy hot water bottle at her feet, put there by her older sister.

Thoughts of Chati and the life she had lost, as well as the upcoming job interview, tugged at Louisa's tired mind, but tonight felt slightly different and with a sense of relief she slipped into a deep, well needed slumber.

CHAPTER THIRTEEN

"Your CV was a little thin on the ground so I'll need to know a few more things," said Grant, clearly loving his position of authority.

He was in his mid-thirties, good looking and seriously camp. He wore a pair of braces over a grey granddad shirt and sported an enormous quiff, held up by a third of a can of hair spray.

Louisa felt queasy. *Probably interview nerves*, she assured herself.

Her CV had been typed up in the space of 10 minutes on Bill's computer. Admin was never her strong point.

"Well, what else can I tell you?" said Louisa gently, searching her mind for ideas. *Don't lie*, she thought.

"I've just returned from six months in Dubai where I regularly helped at an exclusive members club bar," she lied.

Grant was impressed.

"Oh really?" he asked. "What kind of drinks did you serve?"

"Mainly champagne and cocktails, but our clientele came from all over the world so we would get requests for various beers and whiskies, all sorts really."

Louisa was alarmingly good at weaving convincing tales.

"Did you serve food?" Grant asked, holding his pen just millimetres above his sheet of paper, ready to jot down her answer immediately.

"Yes," she replied enthusiastically. "We served food all day round. The chef came from Italy and was really well-known." The lies escalated.

"What was his name?" asked Grant, ready to accept any answer she gave.

"Gino," she batted back without fear. "Roberto. Gino Roberto."

"OK, well, I don't think there is much else to talk about, Louisa," said Grant smiling. "I'd like to give you a chance in the restaurant. Our customers are quite well off, sophisticated people and we are looking for someone with your experience and your graceful look."

Louisa grinned with relief, then paired it back a little to maintain her "grace".

"Thank you, that's wonderful. When can I start?"

In truth, it had been a decade since she worked behind a bar or served food, and she hadn't been all that great at it, but with jobs thin on the ground and no office skills to call upon, this was her only hope.

"If you can just give us the name and contact details of your reference then I'll get you set up on our books," said Grant, turning the paperwork around and handing Louisa the pen.

Shit, she thought. *I wasn't banking on this. I'll just have to give a false email address and hope for the best.*

She scribbled Mike Madden, m.madden@hotmail.com and shyly handed the papers back.

"We'll probably not need them, but it's just a box we need to tick," he revealed with a comedy over-the-top smile.

Thank god for that, Louisa thought.

She was asked to begin in two days' time. She felt a huge surge of relief and pride as she left the upmarket eatery, having succeeded at her first job interview in years.

It was a mild, sunny day down by the river in Inverness. Louisa bought a sandwich from the newsagents on the corner and sat at a bench watching the water flow. She nibbled at the bread slowly, still feeling a little off, and watched a couple lying on the grassy bank, holding hands and looking at the clouds. She thought it was sweet.

After several more bites, she put the sandwich back in the packet, unable to eat more for fear she would be sick. She downed half a bottle of cherry cola and thought it was a heavenly elixir, quenching her desperate thirst.

Suddenly, like a kick to the stomach, a thought hit Louisa and sent a rush of nerves all through her body.

When was my last period? I can't remember.

Her face grew hot, as though her cheeks had been rubbed with a hot towel. Her breath was short with panic.

This can't be happening. I've just got a stomach bug or something. And the late period will just be down to the stress of splitting up and moving. That happens to women all the time.

Even as the words were forming in her mind, she knew they were hollow. Louisa began to walk, quickly, towards the bridge into the city centre, thrusting her half-eaten lunch in a bin as she went.

She marched, fast and fearful, to the nearest pharmacy and nervously paid for a pregnancy test, unable to make eye contact with the sales assistant.

She slipped the test into her bag and marched onwards to the shopping centre to find the public toilets. Louisa needed to know the result right away. If it was positive, she had a whole lot of planning and worrying to do. If it was negative, she could breath properly again.

In the comfort of a tiny cubicle, Louisa sat on the closed toilet and watched her urine drift across the window of the plastic test stick. It stained the first line pink and sent her stomach flipping. *The first line is supposed to turn pink,* she reminded herself. *It's the second line I need to worry about.*

She watched in horror as the second line appeared in bold, unmistakable dark pink.

She let out an involuntary groan of panic, then suddenly remembering she was in public slapped her hand across her mouth to silence herself as she stared, and stared at this simple piece of piss-drenched plastic.

What the hell am I going to do? was her first thought. *I can't tell a soul. Everyone will be so disappointed in me, AGAIN.*

She rested her head on the cubicle wall and sobbed quietly until her chest hurt, and then cried a little more. A woman asked if she was OK, but Louisa's head was spinning and she was unaware of anyone else at this point. Her thoughts were a murky, swirling mess of anger, fear and shame.

After twenty minutes of self-loathing, her thoughts turned a corner as she realised just what was inside her. It was, without doubt, Chati's child. Justin hadn't touched her in months. The day before flying home to Scotland was the very last time she had spent time alone with Chati. They made love and said their good byes with Louisa crying and Chati close to tears. They had been oblivious to the fact that in those final moments together they had created a life.

Chati means life, thought Louisa, crying and smiling at the same time.

She decided this was a precious gift and no matter what troubles lay ahead, she would do whatever it took to honour the life she was nurturing. Her parents, her sister, her new boss... they would all just have to accept it.

CHAPTER FOURTEEN

"Hooray!" cheered Mari as Louisa opened the flat door.

She was holding a bottle of cava and making a victory fist in the air.

"Thank you," said Louisa, mustering as much energy as possible. She had fixed her eyeliner after the flood of tears (having bought a new one in the shopping centre earlier just for that purpose) but was aware the skin around her eyes felt tender and probably looked pink.

"You look awful," Mari said, dropping her arm to her side. "Sorry, I don't mean ugly, just tired or ill. What's up?"

"Oh, I felt a bit ill earlier, must have been a dodgy sandwich but I'm fine now," she lied. Lies were the theme of the day, it seemed.

"Well, let's get some cava and crisps in you and see if that does the trick," said Mari popping the cork before Louisa had a chance to object.

Eventually, she said: "You have, but I'll give it a miss, thanks."

"You've just got a new job, Louisa, we NEED to celebrate this," insisted Mari, already pouring into two glasses.

Louisa smiled and agreed politely, aware of the no drinking in pregnancy rule as she took her first miniscule sip. She waited until Mari went to the toilet to tip hers down the sink.

"Let's get dolled up and go out!" cried Mari as she returned. "I'm so in the mood for a proper blow out of a night. It's been ages since I got drunk."

"Oh, I'm still not quite right," said Louisa, hoping Mari could be persuaded to watch some telly instead.

"Oh, come on, we haven't been out together yet," said Mari, who was so eager to party there would be no persuasion on this occasion.

An hour later and Louisa was fake-sipping her second glass while curling her hair with heated tongs, sitting at the dining table. She heard Mari's high heels clip-clopping on the vinyl floor before she could see her. Mari nervously emerged from behind the door to reveal her figure-hugging burgundy dress, the one she had previously hidden for fear of showing off.

"Wow," exclaimed Louisa. "You look amazing. Where have you been hiding that cleavage?"

"Is it too much? Do I look like slutty?" asked Mari anxiously.

"Not at all," her sister insisted. "It's really glamorous. I've never seen you look so good."

Mari smiled shyly and took a swig from her glass, draining the last drops of cava.

"I regretted never wearing this for Johnny," she revealed. "I just felt so self-conscious, but I figure, I've nothing to lose. I'm not getting any younger so I may as well try and find some confidence and stop holding back… before I'm old."

"Exactly!" said Louisa with genuine joy for her sister. "You're still young. This is the Mari I've been longing to see."

Mari poured another drink and frowned to see Louisa's glass still full.

"Drink up!" she ordered.

"I am," lied Louisa.

Louisa was wearing a short black, sleeveless dress - her fallback outfit for nights when she just wasn't in the mood. It was an effortless winner every time. But on seeing Mari's transformation, she was inspired to rummage under her bed and produce a pair of red wedge heels and slide some red lipstick across her lips.

"Ooh, can I have some of that?" asked Mari excitedly, enjoying the sisterly bonding she'd shunned all these years.

"You know, it's really nice having you around," she said.

Louisa smiled and replied: "I'm loving being here."

She felt a stab of guilt to think that they were just getting settled as flatmates and their happy little home life was due to be plunged back into uncertainty and scandal in the coming weeks.

Louisa couldn't even bear to imagine where she was going to live when the baby bump took over. She couldn't visualise the baby yet - just the bump. Whenever the question of money and housing popped into her thoughts, she quickly buried it, unable to comprehend it at this stage.

One thing at a time, she thought. *I'll earn some money first, then tell everyone. After that, I can see who hates me the most, and who will still be around to support me.*

Louisa applied the lipstick to her older sister's pout, just as she had when they were 13 and 16, and felt a surge of love towards her. Louisa had always developed more quickly than her older sister, in social terms. She was the style pioneer in their sibling pair, despite being the younger sister. It was academically that Mari excelled. Louisa had given up on her abilities early on, having seen what the competition was. Instead of revising for exams, Louisa would learn the lines of the latest pop hits and spend time discussing boys with friends during fake study sessions. It was never a shock for Louisa, or her parents, to open her poor exam results.

It was 9pm and the sisters took a taxi into the city centre. They started out in a large, brightly-lit pub, Scorpion, which was a favourite of all ages, playing everything from Donna Summer to One Direction, with cheap offers on alcohol.

"Two shots of Sourz please," Mari shouted to the bar tender. She was already tipsy, and not intending stopping anytime soon.

"Mari, I don't fancy doing shots," Louisa said, hoping to dampen Mari's flames a little.

"Don't be such a wuss," Mari retorted. "We haven't been out together in… well, ever really."

"I know, but I'm still not feeling great," Louisa said.

"Fine, have this one, then I won't force you to do any more," said Mari grinning. "And two rose wines, please," she continued to the young bar man.

"He's hot," Mari mouthed to Louisa. Mari was on a mission. She felt different that night. She wanted change to come her way and she knew it was never going to knock on her door. She would have to build a path for opportunity.

When Mari was busy eyeing up some men in the corner on a stag do - she could tell because they were all wearing tutus and 'L' plates - Louisa turned to a young man next to her, thrust the shot glass his way and said: "Here, take this. I haven't touched it." His face lit up and the prospect of free alcohol and without hesitation he downed the green liquid in one. "Cheers. What are you up to later? Fancy company?" he asked Louisa with lust in his eyes. "I'm really busy," she replied impatiently and turned her back to him.

Louisa rarely went on a night out without getting hit on. She had friends, and now a sister it would seem, who were desperate for this kind of attention, but for Louisa the novelty had worn off long ago. She'd met so many disappointing men in her wild years of one night stands and brief, intense flings, that she saw right through their attempts and down the line to when the man would completely fail to meet her expectations. She had written their relationship and break-up plan before even kissing them. She wasted no time.

Mari, on the other hand, had never been chatted up. She'd been on blind dates and met people through work, but never been picked up in a bar. It was an honour she coveted - like the Blue Peter badge she failed to achieve in childhood.

This is going to be my night, she told herself, then noticed one of the stag group was looking her way.

"Oh my god, Louisa, that fit guy in the tutu is looking at me," she said with all the excitement of a lottery winner.

Louisa squinted her eyes to see exactly who Mari was referring to. "Oh yeah," she said, with an unimpressed tone."He looks like a player. You don't want to get involved."

Mari felt it was rich of her sister, one of the biggest players there ever was, in Mari's mind, to make up the rules.

"You don't know that," she said curtly and continued to smile at him.

Mari sipped her wine quickly, as if it was water on a hot day, and couldn't help getting frustrated at Louisa's slow drinking.

"Are you not much of a drinker these days?" she asked, with a hint of disapproval.

Louisa was getting tired of her sister's constant nagging about alcohol. "Yes, normally," she replied, "but I told you, I'm not feeling great. On a normal night I could drink you under the table."

The sisters grinned at each other, avoiding a tense situation nicely.

The butch ballerina approached Mari and Louisa and offered them drinks. Mari quickly asked for another rose wine, but Louisa declined, shooting Mari a look that warned her not to complain.

Mari giggled and chatted with the stag, who was begging her to come to the next pub with his group. He told her she looked gorgeous, which was like a red rag to a raging, horny bull.

"Yes, we'll come, won't we," she said, full of energy, looking at Louisa.

Just get through this night for Mari, Louisa told herself. *She needs this, clearly.*

"OK," she agreed, faking a smile and not wanting to stamp out her sister's joy.

Fifteen minutes later, Louisa was sitting among the men in tutus, as they gawped at her beauty. The club was dark and the music much louder than in the previous bar.

Louisa couldn't bear to look to her right, where Mari was locked in a game of lips and tongues with her admirer, but she didn't grudge her sister the attention.

"Have you got a boyfriend?" asked one of the wannabe ballerinas.

"Yep," Louisa replied, looking away into the distance.

She could work this gaggle of guys if she so wanted. She knew the body language and words to make them weak at the knees, but she was exhausted with worry and not in the mood. Besides, she'd been spoiled. No man would ever live up to Chati's standards. It would take a miracle man to rival his calm aura and mesmerising dark eyes.

Sober, and aware she was on the verge of the toughest months, or years, of her life, she was viewing the drunken crowd from an angle she'd never been in before. Everyone was so loud. *Am I this lairy when I'm drinking*? she wondered.

Everyone looked so young. Louisa suddenly felt every day of her 29 years.

A dance remix of Wannabe by the Spice Girls came on and Mari hooted with glee and grabbed her sister's hand to pull her up to the dance floor. Louisa gladly accepted her hand, keen to get away from the stag party, and away from her miserable thoughts, too.

They danced to the song, pointing at each other and singing along. Mari felt free for once. In her boozy state she thought she never wanted to go back into her shell again.

The song ended and they made their way back to their seats to find the stag party had moved on.

Mari looked devastated.

"Don't worry, there are plenty more fish," said Louisa gesturing to the crowded dance floor, but immediately wished she hadn't after seeing Mari's eyes focus on one male in particular, as if she was a sniper positioning him in the cross hairs.

"Him! I want him! I want a boyfriend," she slurred, the alcohol taking hold. "No, scrap that, I want a *husband*!"

"It's ironic," said Louisa, loudly over the music, "you're desperate to get married and I just stamped all over my chance at marriage. We're moving in opposite directions."

"What?" shouted Mari.

"Nothing," said Louisa.

Later in the toilets, whilst Louisa used tissues to rub away the mess of lipstick around Mari's mouth, Mari grinned like a kid at Christmas and said: "I'm having the best night."

"Me too," said Louisa, dabbing at her sister's face.

Mari wagged her index finger drunkenly at Louisa and said: "You surprise me. I always thought you would try and overshadow me at any opportunity, but you're not! Ha!"

"How could I overshadow you," asked Louisa in surprise. "I've never succeeded at anything. I'm the family fuck-up."

"What? You're gorgeous and you had all the friends and boyfriends when we were growing up…"

"Yeah, when we were teenagers. It's been a long time since then," replied Louisa.

Mari continued: "… and you're gorgeous and you always have these glamorous adventures, living in Dubai…."

"Look where that got me."

"… and you're so pretty."

"You've said that already... and so are you," Louisa said with a reassuring tone.

"I was always mad at you for getting so pissed the night before my graduation that you couldn't come," said Mari, frowning.

Louisa paused then said: "I take it mum and dad never told you the full story then?"

Mari said nothing. She looked bewildered.

"I was so stupid. I had just failed my exams and found out that Kev - do you remember him, tall with long grungy hair like Kurt Cobain? - anyway, I found out he'd gone off with Becky and I was heartbroken and felt like a loser with no future prospects. I took way too many paracetemol, then realised I didn't want to die, but I didn't want to survive with damaged organs either, so I waltzed into A&E to have my stomach pumped. They wouldn't let me out in time for your graduation."

"Holy shit, Louisa," exclaimed Mari, leaning in for a hug. "If I'd known that I wouldn't have resented you so much all this time."

Louisa looked a little taken aback.

"If I'd known you resented me that much, I'd have told you sooner," she said with a tiny touch of sarcasm.

"How about we get some chips and go home, while we're still ahead of the game?" coaxed Louisa temptingly.

"What about men though? I haven't met anyone properly yet," said Mari with a pleading tone.

"Mari, you're not going to meet your future husband here. Trust me. It's full of young boys who just want a ride."

Mari laughed, knowing Louisa was talking from experience.

"OK. I fancy chips and cheese!" she declared excitedly.

Louisa was ravenous. What she really wanted was tempura battered prawns and sweet chilli sauce, but there would be no chance of finding that at this time of night. She wondered if it was a craving. She settled for chips and flagged down a taxi.

Mari giggled and lost her high heel as she was tumbling into the car.

"I'm alright, it's alright. I've found my shoe!"

The taxi driver was relieved to see at least one of them looked sober.

Louisa gave the address and the sisters ate their chips like ravenous sea gulls at a bin. The taxi driver usually told people off for eating but decided to leave the women to their feast. It was easier than making small talk, he thought.

Back at the flat, Louisa handed Mari some make-up remover wipes and Mari dabbed her face repeatedly in the same spot until Louisa took hold of the wipe and rubbed her sister's face all over.

"You don't want to go to bed with make up on," she said in a soothing voice. "You'll get all spotty."

Clean-faced and tired, Mari staggered through and collapsed on top of her duvet and fell instantly asleep. Louisa threw a blanket over her then went for a shower.

Even though it was late at night, she wanted to feel clean. She hoped it would help her sleep. From sheer exhaustion, all thoughts and worries were pushed to the back of her mind for the best sleep she'd had in weeks.

The next morning, Louisa rose before Mari and made bacon rolls and tea. The delicious scent had coaxed Mari out of her room, hungover and croaky.

She had been unaware that Louisa was stone cold sober the night before and assumed Louisa was in a similar state.

They settled down to a DVD of My Girl, their favourite childhood film, ate their breakfast, followed by some chocolates and barely moved for hours. It was blissful.

CHAPTER FIFTEEN

Mari held her phone inside her handbag to check her messages. Sleazy Steve always nagged if he saw her with her mobile on work time, and he seemed to have a knack for appearing in her office at exactly the times she was texting, making it look more frequent than it really was.

"Phone, Mari!" he would bellow. "I'm not paying you to text your pals."

At least if it was still in her bag she could pretend she was searching for something if he popped his irritating head in the doorway.

She opened her emails folder on the phone to see the fourth job rejection this month. In a huff, she locked the phone screen and thrust her bag back down under the desk.

I'll never get out of this place, she thought, feeling deflated.

Just then she could hear Steve's footsteps in the corridor, making his way to her office. The hurried tapping of his super shiny leather shoes was a giveaway. Mari glanced at the clock. It was 10.45am, which surely meant this was the summons to collect food for all the shop floor staff. Mari decided to try something she never had before and immediately picked up the phone receiver from her desk and launched into an imaginary conversation.

"Yes, we need two of those cartridges please," she said formally, adding for effect: "what's your cheapest price on those?" She knew this would appeal to Steve's stingy sensibilities. He nodded approval at her and turned on his heel to ask a junior member of staff to fetch the bacon butties instead.

Mari felt elated. She hadn't studied business to end up fetching food.

What often made it worse is that she'd return to her office, stinking of 'eau de deep fat frier' to eat a tub of sliced fruit because she was constantly watching her weight. It was about time the greasy task was passed on to someone else, and for once Mari had the guts to make a change. She felt powerful.

A few spread sheets later, lunchtime came - the highlight of Mari's day, a chance to escape the confines of the beige office.

She walked through the shop, weaving her way through displays of arm chairs and coffee tables towards the bright sunshine beyond the automatic doors. At only one chair away from the door, she heard flirtatious laughter and without thinking turned her head to look. A new sales assistant, Angie, who was about nineteen, was smiling and peering up into Johnny's eyes as he animatedly told her a story, no doubt from his back catalogue of drunken dilemmas in Greece. Mari felt a sharp stab of jealousy, though she had no desire to go back to that relationship full of poisonous paranoia and disappointment. An imaginary image of Johnny and

Angie having rampant sex on the sofa next to them flashed through Mari's mind. She knew all his moves and could picture his facial expressions.

She shook the image out of her thoughts and burst out of the doors, lapping up the fresh air.

She wandered aimlessly around a clothes shop, bought some moisturiser in Boots, then, on a whim, walked into the small salon on the ground floor of a hotel adjoining the retail park and asked for an on the spot cut.

As Shelly cut away around five inches from Mari's chestnut locks, excitement simmered inside Mari. The hairdresser ran some hot straighteners through the finished chin-length bob then angled a mirror behind Mari's head to show off the steep angle at the nape of her neck. It was the most bold haircut Mari had opted for in all her 32 years. She loved the breeze on her neck and the relished that weight had literally been lifted off her shoulders.

As she returned to work, Johnny was chatting to a customer near the entrance - an elderly gentleman, who did not require the "sex stare" from the super sales man.

Johnny's eyes were diverted to Mari, with her slick new haircut, which made her walk with more confidence. He lost his words for a second, which sent thrilled ripples through Mari's body.

You can look, Johnny, but you can't touch, she thought triumphantly.

CHAPTER SIXTEEN

Louisa sat at the small table in her room, furiously scribbling ideas of items she could make to sell on websites such as Ebay and Etsy.

On her list so far were padded hanging decorations, such as a string of stuffed fabric hearts or stars; cushion covers made from old Arran jumpers (she would have to acquire from Bill's wardrobe sometime); and jewellery purses and rolls made from old blouses, of which she had plenty.

It was only a few hours until her first shift at Banks restaurant. She was sick with nerves, or pregnancy hormones, she couldn't distinguish one ill feeling from the other. She had eaten some dry toast with a cup of tea, but couldn't stomach anything else.

Louisa found a floral shirt at the back of a drawer and began cutting it into six identical heart shapes, then stitched them together into three double-sided hearts, by hand, leaving a small gap ready for stuffing later. Cramp pains stiffened her fingers after a while, but she was satisfied with her neat work and thought that if she could make a few of these every week it could add up - maybe only to the equivalent of a couple of packs of nappies a week, but at least it would be something.

Two o'clock arrived, the start of her shift, working from afternoon right through to the close of evening meals.

She entered the modern building, with huge glass windows overlooking the river. Shiny dark wooden booth-style tables with leather benches lined the window-side of the room, with smaller square tables and chairs on the inner section, close to the black marble bar.

"Louisa, darling," cried Grant. "Welcome! This is Sasha, Tim and Megan," he added, pointing to the good-looking waiting staff folding napkins at a cutlery station. They each politely smiled and waved.

"I'll introduce you to the kitchen guys later," he continued. "Come with."

He practically sprinted through the swing door to the staff quarters, leaving Louisa trotting after him.

Grant handed her a pile of smart grey shirts and a long black apron - her uniform. She changed into it and was shown the ropes briefly behind the bar.

"We'll start you off on drinks," said Grant, "until you're ready for tables."

A few tables filled up over the first hour. Two smart women in their forties, sipped white wine and ordered a sharing plate of cold meats, cheese and olives.

Wine was easy, thought Louisa, eyeing the optics full of exotic spirits nervously, *I hope no-one orders anything too elaborate*.

A family of women - grandmother, mother and baby - took up a window booth for coffees and a rustic pizza to share. The baby grabbed the sugar packets from the centre of the table and sucked three at once.

Louisa struggled with the coffee machine behind the bar, unsure of which tap to place the cups under, until Grant came along, sporting a disapproving frown, and muttered: "How did you make your coffees in Dubai? By milking a camel into some Nescafe?"

Louisa blushed with humiliation. She was beginning to feel hungry and weak and there was still six more hours to go.

"Tim, you're back on bar!" he bellowed. "Make sure Louisa's orders go out up to standard, OK?"

He pranced off, clipboard in hand, leaving Louisa feeling useless.

Tim was friendly, with a Buddhist-like air of calm, and happily walked Louisa through every step of her drinks orders for the next two hours. She poured cappuccinos, whiskies, proseccos, mint teas, diet colas, red berry speciality ciders and craft ales. She was getting comfortable, and although the waiting staff were forming queues at the bar for her slow service, there was a steady improvement as each hour passed.

Maybe this won't be too bad, Louisa consoled herself, dishing out a mental pat on her own back.

Louisa left the bar to collect empty glasses from tables and was serenaded by the cooing baby.

"He likes you," said the baby's mum with pride.

He's probably high on sugar, Louisa thought, eyeing the mound of mushy sucked sachets on the table.

She stared into the baby's huge blue eyes, feeling a mixture of fear and fondness. Other people's babies were cute, but what would it be like to have one constantly glued to your hip, she wondered.

Break time arrived and Louisa was offered a choice of food from the kitchen. She wolfed down a bowl of chicken and pasta in a creamy sauce and felt instantly better and ready for the last few hours of the shift.

At 7pm, two men in business suits sat down for a meal and shared a bottle of red. Louisa guessed they were both in their late thirties and both sported fashionable trimmed beards.

Louisa became aware they were talking about her, as the one with trendy glasses lowered his specs for a better look in her direction.

Being watched when she was on the other side of the bar was familiar to Louisa, but in these alien surroundings as an employee, she felt suspicious. She wondered if they were criticising something she'd done. Had she sent the wrong wine? She checked the order slip that had been crucified on the little spike beside the cash register to confirm it was definitely a South African cab sauv they ordered.

A short time later, the man in the specs approached the bar.

"Tell me," he said confidently, "what's a stunning girl like you doing working behind a bar?"

Louisa kept her cool. "It's a long story," she said.

"I'd like to hear it sometime," he responded, smiling.

Louisa began to panic. He was everything she would normally go for - gorgeous, smartly dressed... looked like he had a good income. Her mind was screaming *yes, yes, I'll go anywhere with you*, but she knew it would be wrong in her biological state. Who *would want a woman carrying someone else's child and all the chaos that comes with that*? she thought.

Louisa struggled to find her words.

"It's very tempting, but it's not a good time for me," she told the handsome stranger.

"That's a shame," he said gently, sliding his business card onto the bar directly in front of her. He gave her a smile and said: "Oh, I actually came up to order another bottle, please."

He shyly returned to his table looking slightly emotionally injured.

She was emotionally torn.

Would it be too slutty to see him just once, to take my mind off Chati? she asked herself. *Yes! You're up the bloody duff!*

Regardless, she snatched the card and hid it in her apron pocket.

The rest of the shift went smoothly, aside from a minor episode of over the top hysteria when Grant noticed a typo in the new lunchtime menus he was preparing to launch the next day.

"Don't worry," whispered Tim to Louisa, "this is normal, for Grant. He gets upset at minor things and then gets over it really quickly."

The diners all left and Louisa was asked to give the bar a clean and load the glass washer before leaving.

She was absolutely exhausted but pleased with her progress. She caught a bus which stopped only a three-minute walk from the flat.

When she eventually got in and entered the living room, Mari was there watching TV.

"Your hair!" Louisa exclaimed. "It's fab."

Mari beamed with pride. "Thanks. Do you really think so? You're not just saying it?"

"No, no. It really suits you," responded Louisa with enthusiasm, moving forward to stroke it. "I'm impressed."

"Want a cuppa?" her sister asked.

"I would kill for one," said Louisa, collapsing on the sofa. "So what inspired the hair?"

Mari went about making the tea at the other end of the room and looked over at Louisa thoughtfully.

"I just needed a change," she said. "I hate my job, I feel numb there, and I have the added dread of having to see my ex there every day. But, I've stopped moping about Johnny, really" she said turning on a huge smile. "I think this is going to be our year, Louisa."

"You think?" Louisa asked flatly.

"I think we're going to find the things we want."

"Let's hope so," said Louisa with a stab of guilt at the secret she was harbouring. *I'm hiding a living being*, she thought. *There's a third life sitting here in this room, and only I know about it.* The thought blew her mind.

Mari finished making the tea and brought it over to sit with her sister.

"Do you ever miss Justin?" Mari asked softly, hoping not to bring up any sadness.

"No," Louisa replied. "Not Justin."

She realised instantly she'd given away more information in that statement than she had intended.

"Oh?" said Mari with surprise. "Who then?"

Louisa sighed and looked Mari in the eyes. "You really want to know?"

"Of course I do," Mari replied. "You're my sister. I want to know all about you."

Louisa was touched. She was also afraid Mari would judge.

"Well, it's that guy you'll no doubt have heard about from mum or dad. The caretaker."

"What was his name?" Mari asked.

"Chati," said Louisa awkwardly, feeling her stomach twitch just to say his name.

I'm having his baby, she longed to say out loud.

111

"Was he single?" Mari asked.

"Yes," Louisa replied. She wasn't giving much away.

"Did you fall in love with him?"

There was a long silence. Louisa suddenly broke down. The tears flowed and she began to spit out the words:

"I really did. I hardly got to know him, but I think about him all the time. I wish I could see him again."

She clung to her big sister, who wrapped her arms around her.

"I'm so sorry, Louisa. I didn't mean to upset you."

"It's OK," she sniffed. "It's actually good to get this out. I've been keeping it all in for ages. I'm a mess."

"Why couldn't you start a new relationship with this Chati when you and Justin broke up? Don't you have his email or is he on Facebook?" Mari quizzed, whilst stroking Louisa's back.

"I don't have anything," Louisa replied. "I wouldn't know where to begin."

It was on the tip of her tongue to tell Mari her big secret, but she decided to wait until she'd been to the doctors' surgery and got her head around it before dragging anyone else into the mess.

They finished their teas, gave each other one last hug and went off to bed – Louisa looking as though she'd been stung in the face by 100 bees, all blotchy and red from the crying.

Both sisters drifted off the sleep with images of men from their pasts taunting them.

CHAPTER SEVENTEEN

Louisa's shifts were going well – so well, in fact, she'd moved on to taking orders at tables – and she had an appointment booked for the following week at the medical centre. She felt like a government spy when phoning the surgery to ask for the appointment, wishing she could reveal her pregnancy in code in case anyone would reveal her status to the outside world. But she was relieved to be making some sort of progress, however secret it was.

She'd also posted pictures of two fabric room decorations online with the hope of selling them for £5 each. One sold within just a couple of hours, spurring Louisa on to design more accessories. With her creative juices flowing, she had a tartan, punk-style garter belt in progress next.

Mari was also feeling optimistic and had applied for several more jobs, blowing kisses to each email for luck before clicking send.

The sisters were eating scrambled egg on toast at the dining table, with weekend morning television on in the background.

"I wish I could make eggs Benedict," said Mari, pointing at a delicious-looking portion on screen.

"It just showed you how," said Louisa cheekily.

Mari shot her a frown and joked: "Right, no more scrambles for you."

The phone rang. Both women looked startled. Nobody called the landline anymore apart from their parents, or granny June. It was their mobile phones which buzzed and rang these days. They barely recognised the tune coming from the handset.

"Mum," said Mari confidently as she got up to find the cordless phone in the hall.

"Hello?" she said.

"Mari?" said Nancy.

"Mum! We thought it would be you. How's the holiday going? You must be due home."

"Don't worry," said Nancy slowly, which immediately worried Mari, "but we're at the hospital."

Mari sat back down and put the phone between the plates, saying: "I've put you on loudspeaker, mum. Louisa's here too."

Louisa grew concerned, seeing Mari's tense expression.

"Your dad's had a heart attack."

Both sisters drew a sharp intake of breath. Mari grabbed Louisa's hand.

"He's OK now," Nancy continued, "but he's had surgery to put stents in his arteries. They say he'll be much healthier now with these stents in, so we've not to panic."

The pair didn't know what to say, and sensing this, Nancy continued: "He's in good spirits and we'll be flying home in a couple of days. OK?"

"Ok," they both replied simultaneously.

"Tell him we love him," Louisa said, crying now.

"Oh don't cry, sweetheart," said Nancy. "That's rich coming from me! I've done nothing but cry since yesterday. I thought he was gone. I really did. Thank goodness we took out decent health insurance!"

"Where did it happen?" asked Mari.

"Well... I probably shouldn't tell you this, but we were in the middle of a little holiday hanky panky," Nancy said tentatively.

"Oh mum!" cried Mari, but secretly relieved at a little lightness to the conversation.

"I've been going over in my mind how awful it would have been if that was him gone, in those circumstances. I bet the papers would brand me a kinky killer, or something!"

Nancy managed a little giggle, which comforted her daughters.

"Anyway, I'll go back to dad now, and tell him you were asking for him. He looks really well, so don't go worrying. This operation has been brilliant for him, OK?"

"That's good to hear," said Louisa, not sure of what else to say.

"Love you mum," she added.

"Love you girls. Bye."

Mari and Louisa pushed their plates away and sighed in shock.

"Poor dad," said Mari with eyes as wide as saucers.

"Yeah, and mum. It must have been really frightening," added Louisa.

"I wish she hadn't told us what they had been doing," said Mari, causing both girls to laugh nervously. They felt guilty laughing, but it helped relieve the shock.

CHAPTER EIGHTEEN

The bathroom was lit by flickering candle light. Fruity scents circulated in the steam and Louisa placed a glass of elderflower-flavoured sparkling water with a lime wedge on the side of the bath. She longed for a gin and tonic, but the soft drink would have to suffice.

It was her night off and her feet and legs were aching from days of standing behind the bar or circulating on foot around tables for hours on end. She wasn't used to such hard work.

She sunk into the hot water, wincing a little as her cold feet stung momentarily with the heat.

After reaching for her phone, which she had carefully rested next to the sink, she sunk back into the bath and let out a long, happy sigh.

Holding her phone tightly in both hands for fear of dropping it in the bubbles, Louisa began searching online for pages about stents and heart operations. She was reassured to read several blog articles about speedy recoveries and healthy post-op lives.

She wished she could be there to comfort her dad.

I'd better wait a while before I drop my bombshell, she thought with a nervous kick of dread. *Poor dad will go spare. At least his body has been reinforced. He might be more able to handle the shock than he would have been a week ago!*

She sat up and placed her phone back on the sink and took a sip of her cool drink. Condensation dripped down the side of the cold glass onto Louisa's hot fingers. It was refreshing.

Maybe this is just as good as a G&T, thought Louisa, desperate to convince herself.

As she lay back down, she examined her stomach. It was shiny and wet, protruding through a clearing in the white, fluffy bubbles. It didn't look any different. She wondered what was going on inside and what the embryo looked like. She didn't have a clue about development and didn't feel ready to join any online pregnancy group websites. She was almost too scared to accept the reality of what was happening to her body – and the other person's body within it.

Louisa's figure had long been her best asset. What would she do with saggy breasts and stretch marks? Or worse… a baggy… Louisa couldn't bear to think of it.

Plenty of women seem to have great post-pregnancy sex lives, she consoled herself, *I'm sure it'll be fine. Not that I'll find it easy to find a man after all this.*

She wished she could have chosen a simple life. If she could be with the man whose DNA was currently entwined with her own, forming another human being right there inside her, life would be so much better, she imagined.

Her heart sped as a loose plan formed. Perhaps Mari was right. Maybe there was a way to contact Chati, especially in this day and age when most people had some kind of online presence. She had nothing to lose.

Louisa reached for her phone and began searching his name on Facebook. Not knowing his surname was a problem - in terms of shame, as well as limiting her search options. All she found were pages in unrecognisable languages with no profile pictures bearing any resemblance to her target.

She tried a wider search on Google of his name matched with the building name of her former home in Dubai. Nothing useful turned up, but an idea flashed into focus. She would write a simple letter. She remembered seeing the maintenance company's brand, Trust, on Chati's equipment bags and uniform. She would address her letter to Chati, care of Trust maintenance, and the apartment block address. All she would include in the letter was her name, her email address and a plea for him to contact her.

Louisa felt a surge of hope. It wasn't completely impossible that this could get through to him. Whether or not he would respond was another matter.

CHAPTER NINETEEN

Bill was sitting in his comfy armchair in the living room when Mari and Louisa rushed in with a get well card and DVD box set of a new American court drama. They hovered above him anxiously, as if examining him for signs of weakness.

"We thought you might need something to watch while you're taking it easy," Mari explained, pointing to the DVDs.

"Thank you," Bill said politely, eyeing the box with uncertainty. "That's very kind."

Mari and Louisa had both managed to get compassionate leave from work to take the bus through to Elgin together to see their father. Grant wasn't keen on letting his newest staff member take liberties so early on, but her reasoning had been very convincing when she pointed out that she hadn't been able to visit him in hospital, so it was important to see him on his first day home. He reluctantly agreed, but put her down for an extra shift the following week.

Sleazy Steve, on the other hand had been very kind and understanding towards Mari, perhaps too kind, as he seized the opportunity to cuddle her. The embrace had only ended when Mari forcefully pulled away, with her hair ruffled up by his compassionate stroking. "Family is important," he had said, placing one hand on her lower back. "Take the day off, and if there's anything I can do…" Mari had shuddered, knowing there would definitely be nothing he could do, other than agreeing time off.

Bill and Nancy had arrived home at 10pm the previous evening and looked worn out.

"Are you OK?" Mari asked, turning to her mum.

"Yes, just a bit overwhelmed," she replied.

"How are you feeling, dad?" asked Louisa, intensely staring into his eyes.

"I'm a bit sore here," he admitted, patting his chest where bandages bulged under his blue cotton shirt, "but other than having to take aspirin to thin the blood for a month, I'm tickety boo." He gave his daughter a reassuring smile. "They say I'm in better health now than before."

They moved the conversation onto more comfortable territory, asking about the holiday.

"Up until my incident," said Bill, "it was a lovely holiday. The sun did us good and we took walks into the town every day."

"Yes, it was just gorgeous there," agreed Nancy. "Lots of stray dogs sniffing at our heels, but otherwise, very relaxing. I could do with another holiday to recover from the hospital stress though." She let out an enforced laugh and Bill joined in. The laughter was mainly for show. They were politely coping with the trauma for the sake of their daughters.

"What I will say," added Bill, "is that when I started to feel unwell, I knew it was something serious, and all I could think about was your mother and you two and how I'm not ready to go yet. I think it's given me a boost, if you know what I mean – a new appreciation of life."

With that, Bill rose from his chair, walked slowly towards Nancy, took her hand in his and dropped down gently onto one knee.

"What are you doing, Bill?" asked Nancy, grinning with surprise and confusion.

"Nancy, will you marry me, again?" Bill asked, tilting his head up to gaze into his wife's eyes.

"Yes, of course!" she shrieked. The couple kissed and their daughters moved forward to join them in exchanging hugs.

"Look at the state of me," said Bill, wiping his eyes with a cloth handkerchief. "It's a good job nobody can see this."

"That was so lovely," said Louisa, sniffing and dabbing her eyes. "You two are perfect together."

Mari squeezed her sister's hand.

"Champagne!" announced Nancy rushing to the kitchen.

When she returned with a tray of glasses and a bottle of bubbly - Nancy always had a back-up stash of bubbly - she said excitedly: "We'll have to get planning something lovely and invite all the family."

Bill groaned, and mocked: "I forgot about all that, let's not bother," but smiled at his wife to reassure her he was teasing.

"Ooh, I'm going to get the most fancy outfit I've ever owned," said Nancy, brimming with joy. "Do you think I could get away with one of those giant lit-up dresses from that gypsy wedding programme?" she teased, winking at Louisa.

The McAllisters clinked glasses and said cheers to the forthcoming second wedding.

Louisa savoured the tangy taste of the alcohol. Having searched numerous websites to find out what the rule on drinking in pregnancy was, she chose to side with the opinion that one small glass now and again would do no harm and this champagne was going down very well. It was helping to settle the intense emotions in the room, as well as Louisa's added guilt and nervous energy.

Nancy turned to Mari and said: "Anyway, how is flatmate life treating you? You both look great, and that hair! Good on you, darling."

Mari smiled and said: "Thanks, I needed a change. It's going really well, isn't it?"

She turned to her sister, who nodded and agreed, adding: "Yeah, we've done loads together - decorating, gone out for drinks…"

"See? Out on the pull? What did I say?" Nancy interrupted.

Mari blushed and laughed nervously.

"You should come and see the flat soon. It's looking great," she said, changing the subject.

"And how's the job?" Nancy asked Louisa raising an eyebrow, unsure of what the answer would be.

"Great," she replied, noticing Nancy and Bill both sighing ever so slightly with relief. It irritated Louisa to think they never expected much from her, but then she remembered there were to be more revelations to stay strong for, so she washed her annoyance away with another gulp of champagne.

"I've also been selling hand-sewn items on Ebay," she added.

Nancy gawped at her.

"Really?" she asked, unable to contain her disbelief.

"Yes. Just two so far, but it's something I'd like to do more of and see where it takes me," she replied confidently.

"They're really gorgeous," Mari commented, taking Louisa by surprise.

"Thanks," she said modestly.

Nancy placed a hand on Louisa's shoulder and said with pride: "That, Louisa, is just wonderful. Keep going with that."

"That reminds me," Louisa said, turning serious, "do either of you have any old clothes or blankets I can have to make things with?"

"Oh yes, loads" said Nancy, "Come upstairs." And she led Louisa out of the room.

"There'll be nothing left in my wardrobe when I look later on," Bill muttered to Mari, heading for his comfy chair. "She hates all my golf jumpers."

"Dad, that was really nice what you did there, for mum," Mari said, sitting on the sofa at his side.

"Your mother is the best woman on this earth," Bill said wistfully. "I hope you girls find someone to feel that way about."

He took his daughter's hand and they sat in silence for a minute.

Mari took after her father in the way that neither of them felt the need to fill every silence with words. They were comfortable sitting at peace.

Louisa, on the other hand, took her vivaciousness and constant need for inspiration and stimulation from Nancy.

Mari mused on this thought for a while.

Maybe that's why Louisa and I are getting on so well, she thought. *Oh my god, are we the Nancy and Bill of our generation? Destined to live together in harmony for all time?*

After a small feast of sandwiches and cupcakes, Mari and Louisa said their good byes and walked into town to catch the bus from the station. They deliberately took a slightly longer route so they could walk down Elgin High Street with its concrete fountain in front of St Giles church, which is plonked bang in the middle of the cobbled pedestrianised zone. The sisters had spent their teenage days hanging about there, so it always felt like home.

After washing the dishes, Nancy sat near Bill, who had pressed play on the first court drama DVD already.

"I've never seen the girls look so positive," said Nancy. "They were both... different... don't you think?"

Bill agreed, but didn't give it much thought.

"I think this has been a very good move for them," she continued. "Onwards and upwards."

CHAPTER TWENTY

"Louisa McAllister," called the midwife confidently. To her, this was just another name on her long register.

Louisa shyly rose from her seat and followed the curvaceous women to her clinic room.

"So, how many weeks are you, dear?" she asked.

"I don't know," replied Louisa meekly.

"OK. We'll start from the beginning and fill in all your forms," said the midwife. She was in her forties, with short ginger hair and a soft face. Her pale blue eyes sparkled whenever she looked up from her notes.

"I'm Carla," she said warmly, whilst clicking her pen.

"You filled out some details in the waiting room, which saves me some time, but I'll need to ask you some things that may be a bit sensitive. It's just so we know in our notes what your circumstances are for future appointments or if I have to hand your case to another midwife at times. Is that alright?"

"Yes," said Louisa, who felt like a school girl in trouble.

"Date of last period?" Carla kept her head down facing the notes, but looked up under her eyebrows for a response.

"I can't remember."

"OK," said Carla, clearly disappointed with this answer.

"You're 29 aren't you?"

"Yes."

"OK. Baby's father?" Carla continued.

"He's not on the scene," said Louisa, squirming with embarrassment.

"Don't worry, dearie, we get all sorts in here," Carla comforted her. "Nobody's judging. So, does he at least know about the baby, will he be involved in the pregnancy in any way?"

"No," Louisa responded, faintly.

"Do you have a birth partner in mind," quizzed Carla.

"No," said Louisa, growing close to tears.

There was an awkward silence as it dawned on Carla that Louisa was in a raw emotional state.

"What about family? Have you got a mum or a sister, or even a friend, who is supporting you?"

"I haven't told anyone yet," admitted Louisa, finally breaking down into a fit of tears. "I want to get everything confirmed first, and then work out what to do. It's been so hard lately, I don't know how my mum and dad, or my sister, will react. And the dad lives halfway across the world and I'll probably never see him again."

"Breath," instructed Carla gently. "You're going to be fine. Things always work out. I see this all the time."

"Do you?" asked Louisa, calming slightly.

"Yes. Not everyone has a straight forward pregnancy that was planned with a husband and everything in its place," said Carla. "The fact of the matter is, there is a baby growing in that tummy and we're here to make sure mum and baby turn out just fine, and often families get used to the idea of a baby so quickly. You might be surprised by their reactions."

Louisa sniffed and Carla handed her a hankie from the box on her table.

"We must get on with weighing you, taking your blood and getting you booked in for a scan," Carla said in a business manner all of a sudden. "Can you help me out on the period situation at all? Do you think you've only missed one, or more?"

"Just one," said Louisa. That much she knew.

"Perfect. I can book you in for, say, six weeks' time to scan you at what should hopefully be around your twelfth week of pregnancy," Carla informed Louisa, with a smile.

Louisa felt comforted by Carla's confidence as she went through the motions of the rest of the appointment.

She would get a hospital letter sent to the flat to inform her of the scan date, she was told.

As she put on her coat to leave the room, Carla touched her arm and said: "It might be a good idea to confide in someone you trust before the scan. It's a long time to be on your own with this. Plus, sharing that magical experience of seeing your baby on screen with someone is nice."

Louisa knew she was right. She nodded and left the clinic, feeling a little shaken, but beginning to sense the first stirrings of excitement. Seeing women with enormous baby bumps in the waiting room and posters of babies had hit home that there was going to be a little person in her life. This was no longer about the stripe on a plastic pee stick anymore. It was about a life.

CHAPTER TWENTY-ONE

It had been six months since Mari spent time with her friend Becky. They went from socialising together most weekends, to barely speaking or texting lately. She was ashamed to realise the last time had been just after Becky returned home from hospital with her baby son, who was now sitting on her knee turning the pages of a fabric book and yodelling.

Mari couldn't remember his name, and was afraid to ask.

"He's gorgeous," she said enthusiastically, picking up the lunch menu.

They were at a small cafe in Inverness city centre, having finally arranged a suitable time.

"So, what's new with you?" asked Becky, whilst fastening a bib round her son's neck.

"No a lot, really," said Mari, searching the ceiling for inspiration. "Oh, my sister has moved in with me!" she remembered excitedly.

"Oh, that's good... or is it?" said Becky cautiously.

"It is actually," Mari replied. "We're getting on better now than ever, now that we've both grown up. We're in similar places right now - both single and working."

Becky yawned.

"Sorry," she said. "I was up three times last night with this little guy. He's teething."

"Oh," said Mari. "How long does that go on for?"

"Until he has all his teeth," said Becky with amusement.

"How's Dave taking to fatherhood?" asked Mari.

"He loves it," said Becky, smiling. "It's so cute to see them falling asleep together and playing with toy cars."

Becky continued into a long speech about how her life had been turned upside down by Rory. *Rory, that's his name!* Mari had thought triumphantly, whilst at the same time pretending to be fascinated by Becky's breastfeeding habits and exhaustion. It wasn't that Mari was disinterested in motherhood, she was simply scared to open up to it in case it never happened for her. Besides, hearing about someone else's tiredness is never enthralling.

"The only thing that's been disappointing is that you feel like you lose your friends when you become a mum," said Becky, sipping some water and avoiding eye contact.

Mari felt her heart quicken with anger. *It takes two to tango*, she thought. *If you weren't so consumed by motherhood you would know I've had a relationship and break-up in the space of these six months.*

She made no comment on Becky's remark and changed the subject instead.

"So, I've finally got a job interview coming up," Mari said enthusiastically.

"I thought you liked your job at Williamson's." Becky said, with a confused look.

Do you know me at all? Mari thought.

"No, I've been sick of it for ages," she said. "Plus, it's been worse lately since I broke up with Johnny," she added, pleased to have the opportunity to let Becky know she had life events, too.

Becky simply raised an eyebrow. She was too afraid to shine a spotlight on the fact she'd missed this whole episode in her friend's life.

"Anyway," Mari continued. "It's for a marketing job for a property developer. I really want it."

"That's great," said Becky, with a stab of envy. Her career was non-existent since Rory came along. With Dave working random shifts in the police and no family close by to help with the baby, Becky had felt obliged to leave her retail manager job. She missed it terribly.

"Before I forget," Becky said, abruptly, "it's my birthday in two weeks and Dave will be off work and is going to stay home with Rory so I can finally have a night out!" She threw her head back with joy. "You will come, won't you?" She asked, searching Mari's face for an answer.

"Yes, that sounds great," replied Mari, genuinely pleased at a chance to relive the good old days with her friend. "Where do you want to go?"

"I don't care," said Becky, laughing. "Just out. I want to get drunk and dance. Anywhere."

They both laughed and confirmed it was a date.

"I'll text a few other girls and get a group of us together," suggested Becky. "Shall we go for a meal first?"

"Fab idea," said Mari grinning. "Chinese?"

"Yes!" shrieked Becky. "Let's go for it."

CHAPTER TWENTY-TWO

"Don't just stand there," barked Grant. "Get a cloth and wipe some tables. Never be seen idle."

Louisa snapped out of her daydream about Chati getting her letter and hopping straight on a plane to whisk her away from all this responsibility. In the fantasy they went to a hotel and tore each other's clothes off. Then he surprised her by taking her to a huge town house he'd just bought, complete with a yellow nursery crammed full of luxurious stuffed animals – the trendy, bright-coloured corduroy kind she always saw wealthy mums stuffing back into their babies' prams after being launched onto the pavement.

She fumbled for a damp cloth and smiled meekly.

Grant could be nippy, but he was a good boss in general. Sometimes at the end of the night he would tell everyone to choose a drink and they would sit at the bar chatting for 10 minutes, eating snacks left over from that evening's service, before going home. If Louisa hadn't seen his sociable side, which was extremely charming, she would have found it much harder to take orders from him. But seeing as he was a likeable guy, she happily accepted his authority on the restaurant floor.

With a spray bottle in one hand and a damp cloth in the other, she moved around the room, making each table glisten.

A young man came through the main entrance, holding a pile of fliers.

"Could you put up one of these, please?" he asked Louisa. "It's for a contest we're having at Love Shack in two weeks. We're trying to get as many entrants as possible, but so far there are only two."

Louisa took the leaflet. *Burlesque Battle*, it read. *Winner takes £200. No nudity permitted! Pole and props provided. Simply call 07786445821 to apply.*

"Burlesque?" asked Louisa, laughing.

"Yeah, you know, sexy dancing," replied the man, looking a little flustered.

"I know it," said Louisa, eyeing him with amusement. "Is it just for amateurs?"

"Yes. See the line along the bottom – Am Bam thank you ma'am? That's supposed to be Am for amateur, but I don't think anyone will get it. I told my boss that's not very good, but he insisted."

"I'll check with *my* boss if we can put this up," she said kindly, before he thanked her, waved nervously, and left.

Grant was enthusiastic about the poster and told Louisa some tales about the best burlesque shows he'd seen in Paris, including a drag burlesque act with star of the evening being Carmen Getsome. The pair enthusiastically exchanged stories for a while, Louisa revealing her experience at pole dancing parties with The Wives in Dubai. There was usually an instructor who wore rather disappointing Lycra fitness gear, but she taught them some valuable tricks.

"You should enter," exclaimed Grant, grabbing hold of Louisa's shoulders.

"Maybe I will," she responded with a flirtatious flick of her eyebrows. "I could do with that £200."

She pinned up the flier up in the lobby on the way to the toilets - Grant had deemed it too "tacky" for the dining area - and went back to wiping tables.

Memories flooded her mind of past nights spent seducing Justin in frilly lingerie to jazzy tunes in their apartment. He always said she moved like no other woman he'd ever been with.

She enjoyed the power she felt sashaying around in glamorous garments and at the informal pole parties she had always taken it a little too seriously. While the other women were shrieking with laughter and collapsing in a tangle of limbs at the base of their poles, she was usually swinging round it like an expert, wrapping her long, slim legs perfectly around the shiny chrome.

Maybe I could give it a go, she thought, with a nervous fluttering in her stomach. *I could make a costume myself, easily.*

In a moment of spontaneity, she snuck into the staff room and took her phone from her coat pocket. She compiled a brief text with her name and details and sent it to the number on the flier.

CHAPTER TWENTY-THREE

Having entered the burlesque battle, Louisa became a sewing storm for the next week.

With Mari working 9am to 5pm it gave Louisa hours of private sewing time in her room every morning before preparing herself for the afternoon shift at Banks.

Although Louisa was not backwards in coming forwards, as her mother always said, meaning she wasn't a shy retiring sort, in this instance she felt it was better to keep her secret ambitions under wraps. She couldn't predict how Mari would interpret this. Not so long ago, Mari would have probably criticised Louisa for "strutting about like a slag". She always had a way to make Louisa feel ashamed of her confidence. These days, with a new, more daring, Mari emerging, it was impossible to know. Louisa decided she wasn't going to run the risk of upsetting the happy equilibrium the sisters had found in their home sweet home.

It's better if I just get this contest out of the way without any of the family knowing, thought Louisa. *If it goes well and I win the cash, then I'll spill the beans. If I flop like a dead fish on stage then nobody will be disappointed in me, because they won't know!*

She had a brief conversation with herself, regarding the small issue of pregnancy, and whether or not it would be morally OK to dance seductively in 'her condition', and decided that of course it was OK, because, again, nobody would know. She was getting good at justifying decisions to ease her conscience.

Louisa began Project Burlesque, as she was calling it, by sketching out some costume ideas. She sat at her little table in the bedroom, sipping filter coffee and listening to electro swing for inspiration.

Ideas flowed naturally, like a swollen river after a rain storm, and before long she had a complete outfit laid out on her bed and began determinedly pinning underwear, shreds of clothing and scarves together.

By the end of the week she had a stunning bodice (made using a cream camisole top, stitched onto a cream bra for support) with dark blue satin ribbons at the back to pull it temptingly tight. Attached to the bodice was a removable tutu of navy netting and a long navy scarf, which was so light it would dance to its own beat in mid air. The scarf was attached by Velcro as a long train above where Louisa's buttocks would be. She was delighted with this detail which would provide her with an impressive finale of ripping it off and swirling it around. The fabric alone was enchanting, but paired with Louisa's elegance, it was sure to impress.

With the outfit complete, Louisa turned her attention to music and moves. This part was not so easy. She flicked through several albums on her phone, making a short list of songs.

Lana Del Rey's Burning Desire was sexy, but too whimsical and slow. Marilyn Monroe's version of a Fine Romance was a contender, but in the end Louisa struck it off the list due to its lack of modern edge. Patricia the Stripper, by Chris De Burg, repeatedly teased its way into Louisa's mind but was consistently pushed to the very back. It reminded her too much of Nancy shaking her bosom and belting out the lyrics at every big family birthday party, or car road trip. She considered the stomping rock/folk song Xs and Os by Elle King, but she settled on Just One Dance by Caro Emerald – a sultry, seductive song with hefty brass melodies and suggestive lyrics about a female dancer. It was just right, in Louisa's opinion. It was sassy without any sleaze.

Louisa turned next to Youtube for choreography. She watched clip after clip of stunning dancers draping themselves over rocking horses or huge imitation champagne bottles. She wrote down things she liked, in codes which would help her remember positions, such as: unicorn (one leg bent, her arm straight up above her head); Gene Kelly (swinging around the pole by one hand as if it is the lamppost from Singing in the Rain); and Charlize Theron (striding confidently without moving her upper half much, in a similar way to Charlize in the Dior perfume adverts).

Louisa was building up an effective image in her head of what she wanted her routine to be. It was just a matter of constant practice in her tiny bedroom to make the reality as close to her sophisticated imaginary dance as possible.

She couldn't help but let fear creep in and squeeze her insides – or was it just hormonal sickness?

Mari was also glad of the few solo hours at the opposite end of each day before Louisa returned from work. Her focus was also on bettering herself, but there were no silk scarves or tutus involved. Instead, Mari was writing potential answers for questions she hoped would arise at her upcoming job interview. She also spent hours researching the company online. She wanted to be as prepared as possible. This could be her key out of career boredom... and away from Johnny.

Every now and again she would take a break from interview preparation to enjoy a glass of wine and browse dating websites, but nobody caught her eye.

One evening, Johnny interrupted a session of perusing single hopefuls online by sending Mari a text out of the blue: "Wot r u doin right now? X"

Mari's heart raced. She longed to see him, but knew it would be foolish to undo all her progress of getting over him.

He's immature, she warned herself. *You'll only end up having to go through the whole process all over again if you go back there. Besides, he sometimes pulled stupid faces when we were doing it. Focus on those faces and stay strong, Mari.*

She ignored the text, against all her bodily urges, and gulped another glass of wine for distraction.

CHAPTER TWENTY-FOUR

"Crikey, Mar," exclaimed Louisa, attempting to lift the orange glass recycling tub from the cupboard in the kitchen. It was overflowing with empty wine bottles. "It looks like we've had a visit from auntie Fran."

Auntie Fran was the family alcoholic. She was Nancy's older sister and a formidable woman. If she had an opinion, you would hear it. If a classic song was featured on a television advert in her presence, she would carry on where it finished with bellowing tones, trying to initiate a sing-song, which nobody ever really wanted to join. Occasionally, Nancy would politely accompany her sister out of kindness, with a half-hearted rendition of Big Spender, or such, before discreetly returning to whichever conversation had been so rudely interrupted.

It was not that auntie Fran wasn't loved. It was just that she was only pleasurable in small doses. Nancy was never sure whether Fran took to drink because she was alone, or if she was alone because she depended on the stuff so much it drove her lovers away.

Mari once said to Louisa: "Auntie Fran is like mum on speed, with her social boundaries deactivated."

They both enjoyed a laugh at poor auntie Fran's expense.

Eyeing the bottles, Mari said defensively: "Are you trying to say I drink too much?"

For fear she had hit a nerve, Louisa back-tracked a little: "No. This would only be a few days' worth of Fran's stash," she said. "This probably hasn't been emptied in ages."

Mari cringed, knowing she had emptied it just several days before.

"Some of those must be yours," added Mari, trying to regain some dignity.

Louisa knew, of course, that none of the bottles were hers, but she politely agreed it was possible.

Mari took the box from Louisa's hands and struggled under the weight of it. She rested the bottom of it on her hip and made her way down stairs to line it up with the other boxes ready for collection.

Maybe I should keep an eye on my drinking, admitted Mari to herself. She couldn't actually remember the last day she went from morning until bedtime without at least one glass of wine. *I don't want to become the next Fran – the one Louisa jokes about with her kids at future Christmasses when I show up pissed.*

Mari also noticed her favourite jeans were slightly tight around the waist, which she realised must be down to booze calories, and her skin was a bit spotty. Her body was crying out for her to get a handle on this habit, before it had control of her.

Mari vowed not to touch another drop until the weekend, just to test herself.

Later that day, a beautiful lilac envelope was waiting on the mat inside the front door when Louisa returned from the supermarket. She dumped the shopping bags, which contained about eighty per cent sticky toffee cakes, fifteen per cent smoked fish, a bottle of milk and two apples, on the kitchen floor. What? She had cravings.

The note was addressed to both her and Mari and there were gold hearts and flowers embossed on the back.

Very fancy, she thought as she gently tore it open.

It was an invitation.

Bill and Nancy McAllister request your company at the renewal of their wedding vows at Old Moray Hotel, Elgin, read the first line.

Louisa was smiling as she read the rest. It was only three months away and they were to be at the hotel for 2pm for the ceremony, followed by a sit-down buffet meal.

There was a hand-written note folded in the envelope from Nancy, explaining that there were 20 other relatives invited, including granny June and auntie Fran, and if the girls could wear lilac or purple they could be her attendants on the day. She enclosed a check for £100 so they could choose new dresses for the occasion.

Who uses cheques these days? wondered Louisa. She would have to organise a day of shopping with Mari soon for these purple numbers. Suddenly a feeling of dread thumped Louisa like a mini wrecking ball in the stomach.

I will have a baby bump by then! If I choose a dress soon, it won't fit in three months, she realised.

She hadn't cried for several days, but the flood gates were now open and her well-practiced tear ducts knew what to do.

She quickly adjusted her thinking by deciding to opt for a loose-fitting dress with room around the middle, but the tears didn't stop. She got on with some cleaning, but still the tears rolled down her cheeks.

Louisa even watched some daytime TV through a veil of tears. Her body was doing what it needed to do.

You can't stop nature, she thought, first thinking of the tears, and then placing one hand on her abdomen. *It does what it wants.*

Later that day, Louisa went to the loo and was shocked to discover a small blood stain in her underwear. Her heart raced with fear. Fear that this was game over.

She called Carla the midwife right away and on getting through explained in panicked speedy sentences what was happening.

"Don't panic," reassured Carla. "This is quite normal at your early stage of pregnancy."

"Really?" asked Louisa, feeling hopeful. She felt completely out of her depth, in a new situation of which she had absolutely no knowledge, or prior interest.

"Yes," replied Carla. "It should just be a little spotting, which often happens when the embryo is attaching to your womb lining. If you find it's increasing over the next couple of days or you have any pain give me a call back, but, honestly, this is a regular occurrence."

Carla was clearly used to first-timers who were startled by the oncoming headlights of motherhood.

Louisa felt relieved.

"Thank you so much," she said. "I'll keep an eye on things."

When she hung up, Louisa lay on the sofa with her eyes closed, breathing slowly and deeply, to relax.

Oh my god, she thought. *I was scared I was losing this baby. That must mean I really want it.*

That thought circulated through her system like a warm electrical current, causing her to feel the butterflies of nervousness and love. She hadn't paused to ask herself the question before, of how she felt about the developing child, but this was confirmation for sure. She felt protective of the life inside her. No matter what was coming her way, she knew she would cope.

CHAPTER TWENTY-FIVE

Two days into her self-imposed drinking ban, Mari realised she was more dependent on the relief she felt with a glass of wine in hand, than she had thought.

She replaced wine with fresh grape juice instead, poured into a wine glass, and was managing to resist temptation.

On the morning of her big interview she called in sick to Williamson's.

"Hi," she croaked with several fake coughs thrown in for effect. "I feel awful, I'm not going to make it in today."

It was Johnny who had answered, much to Mari's embarrassment.

"OK," he replied. "I'll tell dad later. See you."

He hung up rather quickly, forcing Mari to feel paranoid that she had upset him by ignoring his text.

Mari had a talent for experiencing guilt. Her default position in life was to look for something to feel bad about in every situation. If she missed a lunch date with a friend, she cursed herself for the rest of the day as a "terrible person", or if she failed to order something from a make-up catalogue doing the rounds at work she would spend the rest of the week going out of her way to avoid the colleague who had brought it in. She once ate a chicken and sweetcorn sandwich in a toilet cubicle on her lunch break just to stay out of sight.

On this day, however, Mari wasn't going to let Johnny's curt reply sap her confidence. She had prepared screeds of notes in an A4 notebook and dressed in a smart white, cap-sleeved shirt with a black pencil skirt and simple court shoes. She had a good feeling about this.

"Good luck, sis," said Louisa, giving her sister a hug at the door. "I'm sure you'll do great."

As Mari made her way across town by bus, she felt a bit sick with nerves. She also worried someone connected with work would see her and pass the intelligence back to the furniture store with haste. She felt bad for lying, but at the same time she was sick of the place and accepted a little white lie was necessary in this case. Or rather, a great big dark lie! There was nothing little or white about faking illness to try and bag another job.

She entered the swanky property firm's waiting area and was told to take a seat by a chirpy, tanned receptionist who had long, bleached blonde hair pulled up into a huge bun, like a bird's nest on top of her head.

Fifteen nervous minutes later, Mari was called into an office by Mr Martin.

He was about 45, slim, with a charming smile.

Mari was taken aback. *Stay focused*, she warned herself. *Never shit on your own doorstep, again.*

Mari vowed never to fall for anyone in the workplace ever again.

Mr Martin, who told Mari she could call him Dan, and Miss Johnston, who hadn't revealed her name was Samantha, sat at one side of a large desk, opposite Mari.

She impressed them with her knowledge of the company and related the tasks of her desired job to many previous experiences and qualifications. Her performance was water tight and she managed to pluck rehearsed phrases from memory in answer to several questions. She walked out of the meeting after forty minutes, feeling accomplished.

She was desperate to have a celebratory glass of sparkling wine, but knew her sister wouldn't join her and certainly did not want to drink alone, after the recent revelations about her ample bottle stash.

She wondered why Louisa had gone off alcohol lately. Perhaps there had been a severely drunken episode recently that had turned her away from drink, thought Mari. She longed to find out and decided to weave this into conversation some time. After all, it was unheard of for a McAllister girl to go tee total without a serious reason.

CHAPTER TWENTY-SIX

It was Saturday – the day Louisa's Project Burlesque preparation would be put into action. Her stomach flipped and tickled with nerves, whenever she did a clock-check and counted down the hours until her stage debut that evening.

She was in the city centre with Mari, on a mission to hunt down two suitable purple frocks for the vow renewal.

The sisters fuelled up on caffeine and sugar at a chain coffee house in the shopping centre before hitting the retail trail.

"It's quite exciting what mum and dad are doing, isn't it?" said Mari, before blowing on her hot latte.

"Yes, it's so sweet," said Louisa.

"Mum will be in her element, planning all this. She loves a party," Mari said.

Louisa nodded in agreement, then added: "Do you remember, though, how stressed she got planning granny's eightieth birthday party? I avoided her for about a week! She was doing my head in."

Mari laughed and added: "She gets a bit too into it. She becomes Partyzilla."

"I wonder what she'll be like this time," said Louisa. "Bridezilla Two!"

Mari giggled and said in a husky, cinema-eqsue voice: "Two people, one love... the only thing that stands in the way of their perfect day is Bridezilla. She's back. And this time, she means business."

The sisters laughed and wiped tears from their eyes.

After a hearty sigh, Mari sensed an opportunity.

"One thing's for sure," she said, "there will be plenty of booze at their do."

She eyed Louisa suspiciously, then added: "I've been cutting down on drinking a little. I don't want to get fat, spotty and miserable... What about you? You haven't been drinking much lately."

"No, I haven't," replied Louisa thoughtfully. "Same reasons as you, really," she lied.

There was a silence while Mari tried to think of a sentence which could open up opportunity to delve deeper, while Louisa desperately thought of a distraction.

"So... purple," said Louisa, winning the race. "I'm not really into wearing purple."

"Hmmm," said Mari, thoughtfully. "I quite like it. I don't suit pale, pastel purple, but the darker kind is gorgeous."

"I suppose," said Louisa. "We might find something that screams 'buy me'."

The sisters finish their drinks and cakes and began the search.

They wandered slowly through a few clothes shops, uninspired and disapproving of every dress they saw, apart from a few that would be perfect, if they were only a completely different colour!

Eventually, in the third floor of a large department store, they saw a dark purple, floor length gown of light, crepe material with a diamante brooch just under the bust. They "ooohed" in unison to see it.

It was fitted at the bust and loose from there down. *That could hide a bump*, thought Louisa, with joy.

Mari spotted a dress of purple satin nearby and tan towards it. She held it up, pleading that they also try it on. It was a knee-length figure-hugging garment, which would definitely have no stretch around the stomach.

"I think this one is much sassier," said Mari, holding the fitted dress.

"But this one says bridesmaid," said Louisa, desperately hoping to persuade her sister.

"We're not bridesmaids in the traditional sense," she said, frowning. "We would get away with shorter dresses. I'm feeling daring!"

Louisa insisted they try on the long gown.

"Fine," agreed Mari reluctantly. "I really thought you would go for the more exciting one."

Louisa stayed silent as they made their way into the changing rooms.

She launched a convincing sales pitch about the elegance of a long gown and the fact they rarely got the chance to wear dresses such as those.

"You can't rock up to a pub in a floor-length gown can you?" she asked. "We can wear short dresses anytime we want."

Mari was coming round to her sister's way of thinking.

"Good point," she said. "I don't remember the last time I wore something like this."

They agreed on the long dresses, much to Louisa's relief and made their way to the bus stop.

"I'm off out tonight for Becky's birthday. Do you want to meet up with us after the meal?" asked Mari.

Louisa could sense a touch of pity in the invitation.

"No thanks," she said. "I have plans too."

"Oh?" said Mari raising an eyebrow. She kept her eyes on Louisa, waiting for more information.

"I'm just meeting an old friend from school for a drink," Louisa said vaguely.

Mari was suspicious.

"That's nice," she said. Then to test her sister, she added: "I could text you late on in the evening to see where you are and join you."

"OK," said Louisa, searching the road for their bus and avoiding eye contact.

CHAPTER TWENTY-SEVEN

Upbeat dance music drifted through the flat as Mari encased her hair in an impenetrable force field of hairspray. She wore skinny jeans and a black lace top, which revealed a little cleavage.

"You look fab," commented Louisa as she passed her sister on the way to her room.

"Thanks," said Mari. "I always get a bit nervous before a night out, so I'm having a little drink before I go. Want one?"

Louisa was shaking inside. It was only two hours until she was due to show up at Love Shack to wait backstage for the contest. She needed Dutch courage.

"Go on then," she said, partly so she could sip a small amount of the drink as a placebo to settle her nerves, and partly to get Mari off her case about alcohol.

Delighted, Mari poured her sister a large glass of sparkling rose.

Louisa's eyes bulged to see it full to the brim. She took a quick gulp and let out a sigh.

"Are you OK?" asked Mari.

"Yes," Louisa replied a little too quickly. "I suppose I'd better get ready too."

In her room, Louisa filled a holdall with her hand-sewn costume and stilettos. Mari had to leave the flat before her, she calculated, to meet her friends at

6.30pm. Louisa could wait until the coast was clear and order a taxi to town. She was too nervous to embrace the bus and let nerves spiral out of control with every stop it made as she would grow closer and closer to the venue.

She'd done so many things like this before, amateur dramatics, dance contests at holiday resorts, karaoke.... but this felt different. There were no friends egging her on and not enough alcohol to persuade her she had talent.

Think of the money, insisted Louisa. *It could be worth the nerves.*

"Bye Louisa!" Mari shouted down the hallway. "I'll text you later."

Louisa popped her head out of the bedroom door and told her sister to have a great time.

Her heart was pounding as she phoned the taxi company.

A car arrived twenty minutes later and Louisa was on her way.

Backstage, which was really just a large office at the back of the night club, given over to the competitors for the evening, there were bowls of crisps, bottles of wine and several huge make-up bags. Sequin-covered costumes and feather boas were draped over chairs and nervous tension circulated the small room.

"Good luck everyone," shouted the club manager over the giggling and chatting. "I'm afraid you'll have to use the toilets to get changed into your clothes if you're a bit shy, but feel free to use this room for everything else. Enjoy yourselves and just go for it. It's just a laugh."

There were a few cheers from a group of rowdy women at the back.

An elegant man, already wearing a black basque with red stockings and enormous red patent leather platform shoes was sitting on the tatty leather sofa opposite Louisa. He turned to her, extended his hand and said: "I'm Andy."

"Hi, I'm Louisa," she responded shaking his hand.

"You look so nervous," he said, grinning.

"I am," she replied with a pained, enforced smile.

"I don't bother with nerves these days," he said casually. "I've performed in drag for 10 years, this is nothing."

Louisa laughed politely and started to ease a little.

Andy proceeded to lift a heavy make-up bag onto the coffee table before him and began plastering a thick undercoat all over his face.

Louisa slinked off to the loo to change into her outfit and returned to find her seat near Andy once more.

"That is gorge," he commented enthusiastically about Louisa's costume.

"Thanks," she said softly. "I made it."

"Bloody hell!" he exclaimed. "Do you do that for a living?"

"No. I just experiment," she replied.

He raised his eyebrows, which were now thin pencil lines drawn over a thick layer of foundation, and said: "Honey, you are talented."

Louisa felt a surge of pride. As she began applying dark, smoky eye shadow, she looked around to see several happy faces, none of them appearing to be nervous, and remembered it was just a little contest. Her fears melted away.

This could be fun, she thought.

***

Mari was spooning spicy Singapore noodles into her mouth furiously, having skipped lunch to save on calories. There were four women sitting round the table, all dressed to the nines and talking at speed about their lives.

"I hope Dave fed Rory on time," said Becky with a hint of anxiety.

"It's your night off, stop worrying," instructed Mel. "When I shut the door on Brian and the kids, I never give them another thought... until I get pissed halfway through the night then I start looking at photos of them on my phone and texting soppy messages! Just leave him to it. He won't go hungry."

"Who? Dave or Rory?" Becky asked, making a joke of it.

It was good for the four friends to catch up after a such a long social dry spell.

"So, Mari," said Becky with purpose. "What was that you mentioned about a boyfriend the other day?"

Mari blushed. "Ex-boyfriend," she stated.

"Sorry," Becky replied.

There was silence as the three women all eyed Mari expectantly.

"Well... it was someone from work, but it wasn't really going anywhere," she explained. "I'm over it now."

Laura smirked: "Was he hot?"

"That's not very sensitive," Becky barked.

"You're right, sorry," said Laura in Mari's direction. Laura was planning her summer wedding and was desperate to steer conversation back round to her favourite subject – her husband-to-be.

"I remember thinking Michael was a dork when I met him," she said, bringing the conversation her way. "But when he took me bowling and was bending over to roll the ball I saw him in a different light, or rather saw his arse in better lighting!"

The women all laughed and seized the opportunity to move on from Mari's relationship failure.

**

Back in the nightclub, the crowd were gathering out front and the manger did a brief running order, giving everyone their number. Louisa would be third, after Andy Adrenaline and before Busty Becca and the Minions (a leading lady with three back-up dancers wearing yellow bikinis, which clashed with their orange tans).

"What's your Burlesque name?" the manager asked Louisa.

"Oh.... erm..."

"Oh come on, you haven't thought of one?" he hissed, causing laughter to ripple around the room.

"Legs Eleven," spilled Louisa, giving herself no time to process the words.

He looked confused but wrote it on his list without hesitation and moved on.

"What's the significance of the eleven?" asked Andy, who now sported a tall red wig and was completely unrecognisable under all his make-up.

"There is none," admitted Louisa meekly. "It's all I could think of on the spot. I can't believe I spent all that time preparing and forgot about a name!"

"Don't worry honey," he said warmly. "It's not actually a bad name. I've heard far worse. Tina Tits was one of the most memorable ones!"

Louisa laughed and was grateful to be standing with Andy Adrenaline. He had a warmth which was contagious. She felt safe.

***

The four stuffed women sat back in their restaurant chairs, surveying a scene of spilled noodles and small puddles of pink cocktail on the white tablecloth.

"Where to next?" asked Mel.

"What about The Fire Pit?" suggested Laura.

"Nah, I think there's darts on in there tonight. Boring," squealed Becky. "I saw on Facebook earlier there's a burlesque night at Love Shack. That could be fun!"

Laura and Mel cheered with enthusiasm, but Mari, who could be a little prudish, was hesitant.

"What's wrong with that?" Becky asked. "It's supposed to be clean enough – no naked ladies gyrating in your face."

Mari smiled and agreed, remembering her personal pledge to be more open to new experiences. "OK. As long as they don't make any of us get up on stage! I hate audience participation!"

"Good evening people of Inverness!" the manager bellowed. "Are you ready for a night to remember?"

The audience cheered. The small night club was packed full.

Louisa's stomach flipped with nerves to hear the enthusiastic cheers.

Andy turned and flashed a glossy crimson grin at Louisa.

"Sounds like a good crowd," he said.

"Please, welcome our judges..."

The three judges - one from a local dance school; one a stylist from a nearby hair salon; and the third a news reporter for the local paper – were introduced and took their places at a small table next to the dance floor, which had been cordoned off as a stage.

"First up, please give her a very warm welcome for being so brave and kicking off the evening for us... it's Satin Thrill!"

Satin Thrill shimmied and cavorted around to Shania Twain's Man, I Feel Like a Woman.

"Shit song for burlesque," Andy whispered to Louisa with a snort, as they listened from behind the door.

The song ended and the crowd erupted into appreciative applause. Satin Thrill burst through the dressing room door, breathless and a little red in the face, clutching her bosom, which had been exposed with large heart-shaped pieces of fabric stuck on to cover her nipples.

Crikey, thought Louisa, trying not to stare at her ample bosom.

Andy was up next. He winked confidently at Louisa as he left the room.

Louisa's nerves returned as she stood there, next in line, listening to Big Spender. Andy Adrenaline received rapturous applause from the audience at the end of his routine, which Louisa so wished she could have witnessed.

"Next, we have a rather beautiful treat for you," announced the club manager. "It is the stunning..... Legs Eleven."

Louisa took a deep breath, pushed the door and marched out to hear the opening drum beats of Caro Emerald's Just One Dance. There was no going back.

Something clicked and it felt as though Louisa had kicked her nerves away like a ball, soaring off into the distance. She felt powerful, suddenly.

With the opening bars, Louisa launched her mentally mapped-out routine perfectly, 'Charlize Theron-ing' along the width of the stage area. The long silk scarf above her bottom trailed elegantly in her wake.

Mari's jaw dropped. She was sitting at a table to the left of the stage, where several feet away, her sister was strutting around in her underwear, albeit the most stunning set of underwear Mari had ever seen.

As Louisa 'Gene Kellyd' her way sensually around the pole by one hand, draping her body gracefully as she went, Mari didn't know how to feel. She was shocked and felt a bit hurt to be lied to. But she was mesmerised by Louisa's stunning package of glamour and sophistication.

"That's my.... that's my sister!" she shrieked to Becky.

Becky shouted: "Wow. She's amazing!"

Yes, she is amazing, Mari thought.

The song was coming to a climax and Louisa ripped off the scarf with her back to the audience, revealing a skimpy pair of lace French knickers under the short tutu. She made a large circle in the air above her head with the scarf, which was quite hypnotic. The crowd let out a cheer and a few wolf whistles were hurtled through the air towards her.

The song ended, almost exactly on four minutes, with Louisa bent over, bowing towards the crowd. The relief she felt was intense. She had given her performance everything. So much so, she had forgotten she was pregnant.

Applause came at Louisa like a tidal wave. She was overwhelmed and made her way back to the dressing room with the widest smile her face could accommodate.

"Sounds like you killed it, girl," said Andy with approval.

"Thank goodness that's over," she replied with modesty, but secretly high as a kite.

Two more acts strutted their stuff and the manager announced a short break while the judges made their decision.

Mari was still in shock. *Why didn't she tell me?* she kept thinking over and over.

"Did you have any idea your sister was doing this?" Becky asked, excitedly.

"None whatsoever," Mari admitted with mild embarrassment.

"I wish I could do that," enthused Laura. "She must have trained as a dancer. Did she?"

"She's never trained as anything," said Mari, bitterly.

"Why would she keep this a secret?" asked Becky. "You must be so proud of her, she looked stunning."

Mari hesitated. "Yeah," she replied, uncertain of what else to say.

The judges made their decision and the manager popped his head into the dressing room to invite all the participants to line up on stage.

The five dancers – plus the three backing Minions in bikinis – stood anxiously in a row while the judges delivered small portions of praise for each dancer.

"Andy Adrenaline, you got the crowd going and added a punch of humour to the evening, Legs Eleven, just wow. That's all I can say... Busty Becca, that was fun and flirtatious, not so sure about your Minions though....."

After everyone had been addressed, the news reporter stood up and said: "There are two prizes tonight..... runner up is someone who really made tonight fun.... it's.... Andy Adrenaline!"

Andy sashayed forward confidently to accept his envelope and blow kisses to the crowd. He was loving every moment.

"The overall winner, however, is someone who blew us away with their moves and the overall effect. Without a doubt, the winner is...." there was an agonisingly long pause – inspired by the many over the top suspense-building moments on reality TV shows – "Legs Eleven!"

Louisa threw her hands up over her face in shock and walked gracefully forward in her stilettos to accept her prize. With the golden envelope containing £200 in one hand and a bottle of champagne in the other hand she raised both up to the crowd in a victory gesture and smiled sweetly.

She was overwhelmed and ecstatic. Andy gave her a huge hug and the other dancers patted her back, kindly. They were all given bottles of champagne as thanks for entering and discount vouchers for a local restaurant.

The crowd cheered as the dancers made their way back to the dressing room and music came on in the club to maintain the party atmosphere.

Mari snuck away from her table towards the dressing room door.

"You can't go in there," said a bouncer gruffly.

"I just want to congratulate my sister," Mari said, with a sweet smile. "She won."

"Alright then, but just you," he said and held open the door.

Mari made her way through the sequins and feathers to see Louisa leaning on a wall, removing her high heel shoes.

"Louisa!" she shrieked, happily.

"What the...?" said Louisa, feeling a kick of nerves to the stomach. "Mari! What the hell are you doing here?"

"I could ask the same!" her sister replied. Mari laughed as Louisa stood with eyes wide open looking terrified.

"You were unbelievable," Mari said, sensing she needed to show positivity.

"Thanks," said Louisa, stunned. "Did you see the whole show?"

"Yes. It was Becky's idea to come," said Mari. "I wasn't sure, but it turned out to be great. Why didn't you tell me though, Louisa? I thought we were getting on really well."

"We are," Louisa insisted, grabbing her sister's hands. "I felt awful keeping it secret, but I was only going to tell you if I won. If I lost I didn't really want anyone knowing. I only did it for the money."

"You haven't lost your job have you?" asked Mari cautiously.

"No," Louisa replied abruptly. "It was just for extra cash."

Louisa could feel a swell of emotion rising within her and didn't want to cause a scene in the bustling dressing room. Her eyes filled with tears.

Mari panicked.

"Is everything OK?" she whispered.

"Not really," said Louisa, wiping away a tear. "Go and enjoy the rest of your night and I'll speak to you in the morning."

"No," said Mari tenderly. "I'll wait for you. We can go home together. You can talk to me about whatever's going on. OK?"

Louisa nodded. She felt sick. She knew her time for secrecy was over.

CHAPTER TWENTY-EIGHT

Louisa wept silently in the taxi all the way home, with Mari holding her hand. Louisa had insisted they go home before she spoke up. She didn't want to give the taxi driver gossip to pass onto his next passenger. Louisa's revelation was for Mari's ears only.

The sisters arrived home and Mari boiled the kettle, nervously, wondering what was going to be revealed.

She placed a tray of hot cups of tea, a bowl of crisps and an open bag of chocolate buttons on the small table in front of the sofa and sat down with her sister, who was still crying gently.

They both sighed, anxiously.

"You must be hungry," Mari said, holding out the bowl of crisps.

Louisa shook her head softly. She felt too worried to eat.

"I may as well just get this over with," she said with a shaky voice. "I'm...." she took a deep breath and exhaled slowly. "I'm pregnant."

There was silence while Mari processed the words.

Louisa broke down into loud crying and Mari pulled her in for a tight hug.

"Don't cry," Mari said. "Don't cry."

She didn't know what else to offer her sister yet. There were too many questions.

"I haven't told anyone yet. I'm so scared," said Louisa. "I don't have a career or a house, or a fucking husband."

"You've got me," said Mari.

"That's very sweet, but you won't want me and a baby sponging off you," sobbed Louisa. "I'll have to find somewhere else."

Mari searched her mind for possible scenarios quickly, in an attempt to calm her near hysterical sister. The thought of Louisa having to ask their parents to live there was unthinkable. Nancy and Bill were supportive, and would certainly accept this, but for Louisa's well-being she couldn't imagine it being a good move. Bill had been disappointed enough when Louisa had returned from Dubai on her own, so to move back in with a baby on toe would be uncomfortable to the say the least.

"Listen," said Mari, forming a lose plan. "I managed with the bills here on my own for long enough, I can manage again. You can stay here as long as you like. We can see if there are any maternity allowances you are entitled to, for food and equipment and so on. You'll get by."

Louisa looked into her sister's eyes. "You won't chuck me out?"

"Of course not," said Mari. "In all honesty, I couldn't face going back to living here alone. It's been so much better since you moved in. I've had more oomph and it's nice having someone to talk to."

"But there would be *baby*," said Louisa, stating the obvious.

Mari smiled suddenly. "I'm going to be an auntie!"

Louisa couldn't believe her sister's reaction.

"You're going to be a mum," Mari continued enthusiastically, not expecting Louisa to launch back into sobbing, saying: "I'm going to be a terrible mum. I don't have a clue about babies."

"We'll learn," said Mari enthusiastically.

To hear the word "we" sent feelings of sheer relief through Louisa.

"Oh," said Mari, suddenly remembering something vital. "What about the father?"

Louisa gulped and replied: "It's Chati. Obviously, he doesn't know. And obviously he won't be involved."

Mari stroked Louisa's back in sympathy.

"Did you not use protection?" she asked, turning the mood a little sour.

"Yes!" replied Louisa. "The first few times. But the day before I left, we had one final, brief... meeting... and it never crossed my mind. I was too caught up in it all."

Mari bit her tongue, aware it wouldn't do any good to cast any judgement.

"I have my first scan in a few weeks," said Louisa, taking on a vulnerable air. "Will you come with me?"

"Of course," said Mari.

The sisters sipped their tea and Louisa felt so much lighter having shared the news and been treated with positivity.

"About tonight," Mari said, "how on earth did you afford that amazing costume?"

"I made it," said Louisa, defensively.

"Seriously?" asked Mari, practically spitting out tea. Her face changed as if a switch had been pressed in her mind. "Sewing," she said with certainty, turning to Louisa.

"What are you on about?" asked Louisa in confusion.

"You need money. You have skills," Mari explained.

Louisa began to understand and met her sister's gaze with curiosity.

"Honestly, the things you have been making lately are top notch," said Mari.

"Top notch!" laughed Louisa. "I haven't heard that phrase in a while."

"Forget waitressing and dancing competitions..."

"Well, I won't be able to dance burlesque when I'm out to here," Louisa interrupted making baby bump gestures.

"...you should sew nonstop and sell what you make. I bet people would pay a lot for the kind of outfit you made for tonight."

"Do you really think so?" asked Louisa, thoughtfully.

"Yes, definitely," insisted Mari. "If you teach me a few basic things, I can help too and we could set up an online shop and launch a marketing campaign."

Louisa began to feel a bit unsure. This was beginning to sound official. It sounded like...business.

Seeing Louisa's worried expression, Mari commented: "Don't panic. I can help with marketing and sales – that's my thing. We can get this off the ground before the baby arrives and hopefully have a part-time job for you in the long run."

Louisa admired Mari's enthusiasm. Mari had always had a business mind.

"OK" she agreed. "If you can help me through it, let's do it."

In the space of just one conversation with her sister, Louisa's outlook had been completely transformed. She had hope, for once, that she could actually make a go of this new life. Her fears of poverty, isolation and humiliation were dissolving. The biggest shock of all was that it was Mari's doing. She had never felt so bonded and so grateful to her sister in all her life.

CHAPTER TWENTY-NINE

Mari spent her Monday lunch break in Mothercare. She had glanced over each shoulder shyly before entering the automatic doors, for fear of being seen by colleagues, but her desperation to browse tiny garments was too strong to be ignored.

She picked up a small, white sleep suit with grey stars printed all over and a matching hat dangling off the hanger. She felt so full of hope. She wanted change and this could be a fantastic new element to all their lives. She vowed to help Louisa through every step, with auntiehood as her reward.

I'm going to be the best auntie, she thought, whilst shaking a pink rattle.

She paid £7.99 for the star suit, hid it in her large, black handbag and went back to work. Life was hitting her with all sorts of surprises lately. She felt different – more confident.

"How's things?" Johnny asked, as she passed him at dining tables. She hadn't noticed him there.

"Fine," she replied breezily. "You?"

He looked vulnerable. "I miss you," he said.

For the first time since their split, Mari felt no guilt or longing. She realised she didn't miss him at all anymore.

"You'll be fine," she said, kindly, and marched onward to her office, feeling triumphant.

She knew he was a mess. She had heard the young sales girls discussing him earlier in the coffee room.

"I snogged him last weekend," said one of the girls, "and he keeps texting me. I mean, he's, like, 35 or something!"

"No, he's not *that* old," said the other girl hastily. "I'd do him."

Mari had shuddered and counted herself lucky for moving on.

With lunch over, she got back to some sales spreadsheets on computer, but heard the buzzing vibration of her phone from her handbag.

She lifted her phone from her bag and upon seeing it was a local number she sprinted to the door to close it.

"Hello?" she answered, out of breath.

"Hello, is this Mari McAllister?"

"Yes, it is."

"Hi Mari, it's Dan Martin here," said the smooth voice over the phone.

"Oh, hi Dan, Mr Martin," said Mari, nervously.

"I'm just ringing to congratulate you on your interview. You impressed us and we'd like to offer you the job."

"Thank you, that is fantastic news," said Mari, throwing her head back in joy and biting her lip to hold in an excited squeal.

They arranged a start date and said their good byes.

Mari jumped around the office, punching the air, before straightening her hair and patting down her clothes to begin typing her resignation letter.

Twenty minutes later, she walked, confidently, out onto the shop floor, handed her letter to Steve with a smile and returned to her office before he could open it, feeling not even a hint of guilt.

Good bye, fools.

CHAPTER THIRTY

"Here," said Mari, thrusting a large black bag full of clothes onto Louisa's bed.

"What's that?" Louisa asked, startled, as it thumped onto the covers and rolled towards her. She was still in her pyjamas, reading a magazine in bed.

"You can make things with them," said Mari. "They're nice clothes I don't need any more. You should be able to do plenty with them."

Then, striding out of the room, she shouted: "There's one more thing for you."

Louisa sat up, intrigued.

"Don't laugh at me," Mari said, timidly, "but you can have this."

She unzipped the black dress bag to reveal a wedding dress.

"Where on earth did that come from?" said Louisa, trying her best not to laugh.

"I'm terrible for buying things on impulse, just in case I ever need them," said Mari. "It was on sale at £50 and I couldn't resist it. I don't want it in my wardrobe anymore. It could be bringing me bad luck with men. If I do ever get married, I'll choose something at the time."

"OK," said Louisa, smiling. She was highly amused by the secret purchase, but after Mari had left the room, sadness crept in. Louisa realised how much Mari longed for someone to love.

The dress was a beautiful garment of lace and ivory satin. Louisa held it up against her body and looked in the mirror.

It wouldn't hurt to try it on, she thought. *After all, I might never get married at this rate.*

She slipped out of her pyjamas and into wedding dress, feeling ashamed all the while. It felt a little bit insane to be a woman wearing no engagement ring, trying on a wedding gown, but as she zipped up the side and looked at her reflection she gasped in admiration. It was too big, but Louisa pulled the dress in at the back and felt beautiful in the layers of luscious fabric. She quickly took it off and changed into her robe to head for a shower.

She had work in a few hours, though she would much rather stay home and get started on a list of sewing ideas.

Louisa also dreaded the day she would have to tell Grant about the baby. She would have to do it soon after her scan, she decided, before she began to show. She wasn't keen on the idea of waiting tables with an enormous bump, but she needed to save as much cash as possible, so was determined to work as long as Grant would allow her.

It had been four days since Louisa's burlesque triumph. She used a small amount of her winnings to buy good quality sewing equipment and storage drawers, plus a tailor's dummy. She found the dummy on a second-hand goods website and it was delivered by

178

a burly man, who kindly carried it up the stairs for Louisa.

"I'm so glad to get rid of this thing," he'd confided chirpily. "It's been standing at the bottom of our bed for a year, watching me sleep! The wife can't sew for toffees, so it was time this lady (he pointed to the dummy) found a new home."

Looking at the dummy next to her sewing table filled Louisa with excitement. *I'm really doing this*, she thought.

Her mobile phone rang. It was the reporter who had judged the contest. He wanted a few quotes for a story about the event, to go alongside a picture spread. Louisa hadn't noticed the photographer at the event. She had been too wrapped up in her routine.

Jack, the reporter, began: "So, where did the name Legs Eleven come from?" he asked.

Louisa pondered this as quickly as she could. The number eleven had been running through her mind a lot recently. If her calculations were correct, the baby would be due in November, the eleventh month of the year. Perhaps that was where the idea came from subliminally. She couldn't tell Jack this, of course.

She blagged an appropriate answer: "I suppose I believe life is a bit like bingo," she said, making it up as she went. "You try your best with the numbers you're given and every now and then you get to shout 'bingo!' when something great happens."

"Interesting," Jack commented while he wrote notes.

"What do you do for a living?" he continued.

"I'm a..." before the word waitress slipped out, she decided to go down a different route, and with one hand on the tailor's dummy she bravely said: "....seamstress."

"Oh really?" asked Jack. "Do you have a shop in town or do you work from home?"

"I work from home," Louisa replied.

"What's the business called? I could give it a plug in the article," Jack said.

"Erm... it's also called Legs Eleven," said Louisa under pressure. She then found herself launching into a business pitch, which felt as if she was having an outer body experience. The words tumbled out freely.

"I create home decoration items," she said, "but also enjoy creating burlesque-inspired pieces." Her eyes searched around her bedroom for inspiration and fell upon the wedding dress. "If a woman has a wedding dress she loves but never wears I can turn it into a burlesque outfit for her to enjoy with her husband. Or bridesmaid dresses that sit in the wardrobe, for that matter. I can take bespoke orders."

She shocked herself to sound so professional.

"That's exciting," said Jack. "Have you got a website or contact details I can include in the piece?"

"Well... you could give them my email address.... and I have a Legs Eleven Facebook page," she lied, deciding to set one up immediately.

Jack took her details and said the article would be in that week's paper.

Louisa felt nervous, but enjoyed the first stirrings of ambition. She had often hoped for career success, but had never found anything she was good at. This, she hoped, was her niche.

Later that night, when Mari returned home from work, the sisters set about creating a website. Louisa was completely blank, when it came to business and technology, but Mari was in full stride. She found a domain name, bought it and proceeded to build a website using a template with Louisa instructing her on colours and typefaces.

"We need some photos of your burlesque costume to put on the home page, so people can see what it's all about," said Mari, "and some pictures of the other bits and bobs you've made"

Louisa set about snapping pictures using her mobile phone. She began to dress the tailor's dummy with the costume, when Mari interrupted: "What are you doing? Put it on."

"On me?" asked Louisa.

"Yes. It will be far more appealing on a good-looking gal than on a dummy," said Mari.

Louisa agreed and changed into the bodice. She posed for several pics, holding the floaty scarf tail elegantly behind her. They chose the most alluring one, edited it to transform it into a black and white, sultry picture and posted it onto the web page.

They clinked glasses of grape juice in celebration when the button was pressed to launch the site.

Mari grinned. "And Legs Eleven, my dear sister, is born."

CHAPTER THIRTY-ONE

"You're a dark horse," said Grant, grinning wildly. "I had no idea you were a seamstress."

Louisa stepped away from the fridge she was stocking with wine and blushed furiously.

Grant was holding a newspaper open at a two-page spread about the burlesque contest. The largest photograph was of all five contestants standing in a row with their champagne bottles. The second largest picture was of Louisa holding her prizes aloft with a beauty queen smile.

The main article hailed the contest a success, raising £600 for charity and there was a smaller article on the second page under the headline: Eyes down for burlesque winner's business.

Louisa was gobsmacked. It looked excellent. Her new website was included, she was glad to see, having stated it in a voicemail for Jack the reporter the day after their phone interview.

Grant gave Louisa a playful shove and said: "Get you!"

The staff gathered round to praise her and look at the article.

"Oh my god, look at that fella," said Tim about Andy Adrenaline.

"He was lovely," insisted Louisa. "He was really friendly."

Louisa was enjoying the attention, but began to feel a bit apprehensive when her colleagues began hitting her with queries about making items for them. They asked about costs, which Louisa realised was something she would need to plan carefully.

Her message board on the Legs Eleven website began to dance with activity as women pleaded for Louisa to transform their wedding dresses into sexy costumes.

After her shift, despite being exhausted, Louisa took a hardback notebook and began listing price guidelines and working out an order form, which she would ask Mari to help her upload to the website, to make requests easier to communicate. She could already envision the threads of conversation getting tangled, causing her to get stressed and throw in the towel. She wanted to do this properly. Professionally.

Mari helped her create a booking system online and her first three orders were confirmed. The customers agreed to send their unwanted clothing to Louisa by post and she promised them postal return of the finished product within one month.

The next morning, Mari appeared at Louisa's door, holding the newspaper article.

"When are you going to tell mum and dad about this?" she asked. "They're coming through to visit on Saturday. I think they'd be delighted to see this."

Louisa smiled and said: "OK, I'll tell them. I hope dad doesn't find it a bit smutty."

"No," said Mari, reassuringly, "It's not like you've got your boobs out in the picture. He won't be bothered."

Mari was about to leave the doorway, but hesitated and turned her head back towards her sister.

"What about the other thing?" she asked gently. "When are you going to tell them?"

Louisa looked down at her hands. "Not yet," she said softly. "After the scan I think."

"Louisa, they're your mum and dad," Mari said, her voice picking up a little in volume. "They kind of need to know. They're going to be grandparents."

"Yes," said Louisa curtly, "I just said I would tell them, but not until I've seen for myself that it's really in there."

Mari shrugged and said: "OK. You know I'm only trying to help."

"I know," said Louisa, and added "thank you", to try and smooth over the tension.

***

That evening when Mari returned home from work she took a cup of tea and a couple of biscuits through to her sister, who was busy at the sewing machine.

"It's looking good," said Mari, gazing at the ivory lace, which was being combined with strips of fuscia pink ribbon, at the request of her customer.

"Thanks," said Louisa, looking up from her task, with a pale complexion and swollen eye bags from exhaustion.

"Louisa, I think you're going to have to leave the restaurant," Mari suggested."You're doing too much."

"But I need..."

"I know you need the money," interrupted Mari, "but you'll make more money if you can dedicate yourself to getting these orders out on time and getting good feedback for the website. You've got to think of the bigger picture and whether you want to turn this into a career, or would you be happy going back to waitressing after the baby comes?"

Louisa knew Mari was right, she just couldn't bear the thought of leaning on her sister financially, until this was more lucrative.

"I start my new job in a fortnight," said Mari, "and I'll be earning more than I do now. The bills will all be covered. I really don't mind. I'm used to it. Get your head into this and make it work. Forget the restaurant."

Louisa's eyes misted. She stood up and hugged her sister tightly.

"I don't know what I'd do without you, Mari," she said. "I keep messing up my life, and here you are acting as my fairy godmother, giving me a chance to change it."

Mari was heartened by her sister's gratitude, but she truly believed this was worth supporting. She had never seen Louisa show so much skill and was keen to encourage it. Any jealousy she harboured for her sister was long gone.

CHAPTER THIRTY-TWO

The aroma of sweet cakes rising in the oven floated throughout the flat. It made Louisa hungry. She barely left her sewing station, whenever she was home, and kept forgetting to eat.

"I wish I had that problem," said Mari, who was always planning her next snack or meal.

"You need to keep your strength up though," she said curtly to Louisa.

"I know," she agreed, searching the kitchen cupboards for a quick fix.

She peeled a banana and ate it desperately.

"Coffee?" asked Mari, switching on the kettle.

"Yes please," snorted Louisa whilst chewing.

Nancy and Bill were due in a couple of hours and Mari had spent the morning cleaning and baking, with the radio on for motivation.

"So, when are you going to tell Grant you're leaving?" she asked Louisa.

"I think I'll do it tomorrow," she said with dread. "He's going to hate me."

"He might give you a hard time," agreed Mari, "but this is for the sake of your future. He will easily find another waitress. Be brave," she added with a reassuring smile.

Louisa showered and put on some smart jeans and a polka dot T-shirt.

Mari was also in polka dots when Louisa returned to the kitchen.

"Oops," Louisa said with a laugh, pointing at Mari's matching top.

"At least they're different colours," Mari said, rolling her eyes.

Nancy and Bill rang the door bell and entered without waiting.

"Hi girls," Nancy shouted down the hallway. "Here's some bits and pieces," she explained before even pausing to receive her welcome, and she began unpacking the food gifts, chatting to herself about what they were and which ones she picked up on special offer. Meanwhile, the sisters hugged Bill and greeted him, before waiting at the kitchen counter for Nancy to finish her display.

"Hi," Mari finally said, with irony, when Nancy eventually rolled up her empty bag and turned to look at her daughters.

"Thanks for the food," said Louisa, her eyes dancing along the line-up of chocolates, dried figs, heart-shaped pasta and exotic fruit juice.

"I like to feed my girls," said Nancy grabbing them both for a squeeze.

They all sat down with coffee and Mari's home-made lemon drizzle fairy cakes.

"Very good," Bill said, sinking his teeth into a moist bun.

"Yes, you'll have to give me the recipe," enthused Nancy. "Delicious."

She finished her cake then rummaged about in her handbag for an envelope.

Handing the envelope to Mari she said proudly: "This is a little 'well done' from us on getting your new job. We're really proud of you. Get yourself something nice."

It was a voucher for a clothes shop. Mari thanked them both and proceeded to tell them a bit about what the new job would entail and how thrilled she was.

After a few minutes, Mari nudged the newspaper on the table towards Louisa. "Louisa has some news too," she said, winking at her sister.

Louisa felt a surge of panic. *Not now, Mari*, she thought urgently, then seeing the newspaper, realised what her sister meant. *Oh THAT piece of news*, she thought with relief.

She opened the paper to the burlesque article and handed it to her mother, smiling coyly.

Nancy's eyebrows lifted in surprise, then she smiled with endearment, followed by a jaw-drop of shock as she read her way across the pages. Bill's curious gaze shifted from Nancy to Louisa, and back to Nancy continuously as he waited his turn to see the paper.

Nancy thrust the article at Bill and stood up to give Louisa a kiss on the head.

"I am absolutely gobsmacked," she said. "I'm so proud."

Nancy looked at Mari, who was grinning happily, and then said to Bill: "This calls for a celebration, doesn't it?"

"I'm still reading it," he said, trying to catch up.

A minute later, Bill put the paper down and said with a cheeky laugh: "You little devil. We had no idea you were doing all this."

"Neither did I to begin with," said Mari, choosing her words carefully lest she walk into a trap that might alert to suspicion to the bigger secret in the room.

Louisa blushed and said: "Mari has been a huge help in setting up the business. She built my website... in fact it was her idea, after seeing my costume."

Nancy was wiping her eyes with a tissue from her pocket.

"What are you crying for?" asked Louisa.

"I'm just so proud to see you both doing so well," she replied, "and getting along with each other."

Bill chipped in: "You're doing us proud kiddos."

He reached into his pocket for his wallet and pulled out £30 in notes for Louisa. "If we had known about your success we'd have put it in a card like your sister's, but here you go. We must keep things equal," he said raising his index finger to make the point.

"We need champagne," said Nancy, glancing at Mari.

"Well... we're both cutting back on drinking right now," Mari said, giving Louisa a reassuring look. "We both decided to launch health kicks."

Louisa was grateful to have an ally, after weeks of going it alone.

Nancy looked disappointed. "I suppose that's a good idea," she eventually said. "Maybe I should do that with the wedding renewal coming up."

Nancy pulled out some papers and fabric swatches from her handbag and laid them on the table, explaining what her colour scheme was and who had replied to the invites so far. She was buzzing with energy.

Bill was reading through the rest of the newspaper by this point. He'd heard it all before. Several times.

Louisa's phone vibrated halfway through Nancy's explanation of which flowers she had chosen and why. Without being too obvious, she swiped the screen to allow the message to come into view. It was an email. Expecting it to be regarding Legs Eleven orders, she casually opened the email and read:

Hi, I got your letter. Chati. xx

"Excuse me," she blurted out and rose to her feet, feeling woozy. "I need the loo."

Mari eyed her suspiciously.

Louisa sat on the closed toilet, her heart pounding heavily.

"Shit, shit, shit," she whispered. She was not prepared for this. Not right now, with her mum and dad in the building.

She began to feel sick. Her mouth filled with saliva which she couldn't swallow fast enough. She turned around and spat into the loo several times, longing for vomit to appear so she could get this dreadful episode over with, but nothing rose from her stomach.

She sat on the floor, leaning against the bath and tried closing her eyes and breathing slowly.

Maybe this is a panic attack, she thought, having never had one she knew of with which to compare it.

What was she suppose to do, she wondered. Did she really want him in her life? As the weeks in Scotland had passed, she had begun to accept her fate as a single mum. She no longer pictured Chati in her imaginary family set-up. The memory of his face, which had until very recently been crystal clear, was now fading.

Louisa focused her eyes on the chrome door handle from her position on the floor. She felt comfort in fixating on a simple stationary object. The nausea subsided.

She remembered the passionate moments with Chati. Those, she would never forget. Then the sight of him playing with the neighbour's child appeared in her memories. She felt calm all of a sudden. She knew what to do. Later, she would have to reply.

CHAPTER THIRTY-THREE

"Oh my god!" Mari shrieked. "This is so exciting."

Louisa was shell shocked.

"Don't you think so?" Mari asked, pacing the room. "You said you wanted to see him again, that you had fallen for him. This could be your chance to get things back on track."

"It's not that simple is it?" said Louisa meekly. "We barely know each other. He's away over there and I'm here, starting this new life."

Mari sat down on the sofa, biting her finger in deep thought. She finally said: "So what? You don't have to marry they guy just because you've sent him an email. All this is, is a chance to open up communication. Test the waters. Maybe all that will come of this is you'll send letters and photos of your child every now and then and at least it (pointing to Louisa's stomach) will know who its father is."

"You're right," said Louisa. "I'm thinking too much about it. I should just reply and keep it simple. I'll expect nothing of it and that way it can't effect me too much."

Thanks for the email, she typed. *I have something very important to tell you. I'm pregnant. I don't expect anything from you, I just needed to tell you.*

She clicked send and felt instantly guilty at sending such big news to someone out of the blue. News that would change their life.

"Don't feel bad," insisted Mari. "Think of how many tears you've cried over this. It takes two to tango, as they say."

CHAPTER THIRTY-FOUR

"Can I have a word with you," Louisa asked Grant.

"Sure, sweet, what's it about," he asked casually, unaware of what was about to unfold.

"I'm going to have to leave, I'm afraid," said Louisa, summoning all her strength.

"Oh no, why?" he wailed.

"The sewing business is taking over and I'm just finding it too much," Louisa explained.

"Why don't we just reduce your shifts?" Grant suggested. "You're good at this and people like to come in and see your smiley face."

She tried several other tactics, such as she needed to help her sister around the house more and spend time with her parents. Nothing was persuading Grant to let her go without a fuss.

"I'm pregnant," she announced harshly with no sugar-coating.

"Are you joking," Grant asked, smiling.

"No," Louisa said, straight-faced.

Suddenly, Grant was in agreement that it would be best for Louisa to hang up her apron before things got "too much" for her.

The rest of the shift was awkward, but Grant agreed she didn't need to work her notice. He had a list of reserves he could call. Louisa was relieved.

She spent the next day so fixated on her first wedding-dress-to-basque project, she failed to notice the email in her inbox for several hours, or rather, was avoiding checking her inbox.

Eventually when she took a break for a hot cup of tea and a tuna sandwich, she felt brave enough to open her emails.

As she had expected, there was a reply from Chati.

I am shocked, but really happy. I knew I would see you again in life. You are special. Are you healthy with child? Are you being looked after? When is the baby to be born? If you are wanting me, I will come to Scotland right away and live in a hotel. I have saved up my pay for a while. I wanted to get out of Dubai anyway. Can I come and see you?

Louisa wept with joy and fear all at once. She was tired of crying. She'd never felt so emotional in all her life as she had done during the last couple of months.

Yes, she began typing. *But only as a visitor. We need to get to know each other.*

CHAPTER THIRTY-FIVE

Mari's first week in the new job had gone fabulously. She felt appreciated and had someone serving *her* coffee for a change. There were no more greasy bacon errands to run.

She was relieved to learn that dishy Dan Martin was happily married and out of reach. She had no interest in a work romance, and he would have been tough to resist had he been on the market and interested.

It was clear that every woman in the office felt the same. They could be grumping about a missed deadline one minute, then turn on the charming smile the minute Mr Martin strolled in. It made Mari laugh, though she knew was also guilty of swooning.

Louisa had completed her first garment, taken photos of it on the tailor's dummy for her website and sent the package off to its delighted owner. She moved immediately onto the next order. Things were ticking along nicely. It was beginning to feel like a job.

She wasn't going to get much work done on this particular day, however, as it was her scan day. As promised, Mari met her at the hospital. Mr Martin had been sympathetic to hear the tale and allowed her to take the company car.

Louisa was shaking.

"Calm down," said Mari. "It'll be fine."

"It's just one of those huge moments," said Louisa. "I'm not sure what to feel."

They were called into the dark sonography room by a friendly woman.

"Is this your first?" she asked, looking at the two women, waiting for the pregnant one to identify herself.

"Yes," said Louisa, her voice fluttering.

She was instructed, gently, to lie down and the sonographer proceeded to squirt warm jelly on her abdomen before placing the mechanical instrument on her skin. It rolled around for a few seconds before locking onto the image of a small, alien-like creature kicking its little legs frantically.

Louisa drew in a breath sharply, in disbelief. She looked at Mari. Tears were reflecting like moonlit rivers on Maris cheeks in the light of the computer screen.

Mari squeezed her sister's hand and Louisa let out an emotional cry.

The baby's head and body were measured precisely and the sonographer took great pleasure in announcing that everything looked healthy.

She printed several pictures for Louisa to stare at for the next few days in wonder. Louisa examined every millimetre of each picture over and over. She would fall asleep visualising the baby thrashing its limbs around, full of life.

She was ready to tell the world. Starting with Nancy and Bill.

CHAPTER THIRTY-SIX

Legs Eleven took off like a soaring jet. Louisa spent a whole afternoon downloading a logo design software package and learning - by trial and error – how to create her own business logo. She was rather impressed with herself to see the finished result – a fancy script font saying 'Legs' and a pair of legs in stilettos as the eleven. She even worked out how to add this to her website. Technophobe Louisa had come a long way in a short space of time.

At lunchtime Mari called from work.

"I'm borrowing the work car tonight. I have a few meetings first thing tomorrow," she said. "How about we head through to Elgin tonight after dinner?"

"Erm... I'd really like to get this outfit finished," said Louisa hesitantly. "There's a really hard little zip. I've been using video clips online to learn how to do it. It's taking me bloody ages."

"I just think...there's no time like the present," Mari hinted.

"Oh," Louisa said. It suddenly dawned on her that Mari had an ulterior motive. "I'm not sure."

"Louisa, it's been a week since your scan," Mari said firmly, but without raising her voice. "I think mum and dad need to know. Plus, it will probably make you feel so much better. What if you start showing soon and your own parents don't know? And you don't want to leave it too close to the wedding thingy."

"Yeah, I suppose it's time," said Louisa with a heavy sigh. "I'll have dinner ready for when you get home and we can leave straight after."

"Thanks," said Mari with satisfaction. "Love you."

She hung up, thinking with amusement about their relationship. She sounded like Louisa's wife.

***

After fuelling up on stir-fried chicken, vegetables and noodles – one of the few meals Louisa liked to cook – the sisters set off on the A96.

Louisa turned on the radio. Madonna's *Don't Tell Me* was halfway through.

She slid the volume dial round further and both women began singing. Their voices blended perfectly as they reverberated off the dashboard. Who cared if they hit a few bum notes? This was car karaoke at its best.

After the song ended, they both sighed happily and Louisa turned the volume down again to chat.

"Do you think love *is* real?" she asked.

Mari's eyes popped. "Why are you asking *that*?"

"The song, dummy. That's what Madonna was banging on about."

"Of course it is," said Mari.

"I know it's real when it comes to your blood relations," Louisa responded thoughtfully, "but there have been so many times I was sure I loved a man but when it all went wrong it was easy to snuff out those feelings and move on."

"Maybe you genuinely were in love, but your brain erased it as a coping mechanism," Mari suggested.

"Possibly," Louisa agreed. "Have you ever been in love - truly in love?"

Mari pondered this for a minute.

"I don't think so," she said, as if realising this for the first time. "I've come very close to it and always wished for it but, usually, I always feel more strongly about the other person than they ever do about me. I give too much to the wrong people."

"It'll happen," said Louisa reassuringly.

"We don't really know that do we?" said Mari. "I bet in a lot of cases, people who are equally desperate find each other and just settle for that because at least they have found someone to be with. I bet they are not really in love, they are just comfortable. Hell, I'd settle for that!"

"That's a bit sad," said Louisa. "I think some people do find a real spark. There are people who are so into each other they always end up back together, whatever happens."

Mari wondered if Louisa was thinking about Chati. Louisa hadn't said very much since agreeing that Chati should come to Scotland. He was due in a week.

He would be staying at the Travel Inn and they agreed to go on dates and take it slow.

Mari was hopeful that Louisa would find happiness, even if it meant Mari losing the best thing that had happened to her in a long time – her flat mate.

They pulled up at Nancy and Bill's house and walked up the driveway, linking arms.

Mari gave Louisa a supportive pat on the back and whispered: "It will be fine," as she rang the door bell.

Bill answered only a moment later.

He kissed his daughters' cheeks and they heard female laughter from the living room.

"Fran's here," he said, rolling his eyes.

"GIRLS!" Fran bellowed as they walked into the room. "You're both looking gorgeous. What's the news?"

Mari jumped in first, sensing Louisa's nerves.

"Well, I've just started a new marketing job, which I love," she told her aunt.

"Good, good," she said, looking at Louisa next for news.

"I've been sewing a lot," said Louisa blankly.

"That's very modest," said Nancy smirking. "She's launched her own business, Fran."

"My, my, that's impressive," said Fran. "I never thought you were the career type, Louisa. I always pictured you as a little dolly bird on some hunk's arm!"

Fran was the only one laughing.

"Well, you've got to grow up some time," was Louisa's chirpy response to break the tension.

Fran turned to Mari and said, with menace: "Your mum told me about that utter ass hole dumping you."

"I never said that," said Nancy abruptly.

"You give me his address and I'll chin him," Fran added with a loud laugh.

"It's OK," Mari responded, blushing. "*I* dumped *him*, and I really don't care anymore."

Fran raised two thumbs up and said: "Men. Ass holes. Except you, Bill, dear."

Bill rolled his eyes.

"Tea, anyone?" he said, desperate to get out of the room.

"It's nice to see you two on a Wednesday night," said Nancy. "What made you want to come through tonight?"

Louisa stayed silent and Mari awkwardly replied: "We just thought it would be nice, seeing as I have the work car tonight, that's all."

Louisa was relieved that Mari hadn't set her up for an announcement. She couldn't face delivering her delicate news while Fran was in the room.

An hour ticked by slowly while Fran revealed she had been attending an alcohol support group.

"I'm not going to kick the habit completely," she said, "I mean, that would be ridiculous, but I just need to know I have control. I realised I was coming close to rock bottom when I drank the sherry mum gave me for Christmas in one night. That stuff is foul. You have to be desperate to drink that."

"Hear, hear," said Nancy, who had also been bestowed with a bottle from granny June.

"Well, Fran, I think it's great that you're taking positive steps," said Nancy tenderly.

"Why? Do you think I have a big problem?" she said, suddenly getting defensive.

"No," said Nancy, growing weary of the conversation. "*You* said you did. I'm merely supporting what you want from life."

"Anyway," said Bill, rising from his seat and saying to Fran. "Do you want a lift down the road?"

Hints didn't come any larger than this.

Fran frowned a little, but said: "OK then. It's a shame I have to go so soon, when I hardly see the girls, but I'll take a lift when it's offered."

Nancy smiled with appreciation towards Bill, who winked at her.

Fran hugged her nieces and sister and was ushered out and into the car. "Alright, Bill, no need to shove a rocket up my arse! I'm coming," they heard her say impatiently in the hallway.

Nancy took her daughters through to the dining table and showed them seating plans for the wedding renewal meal and discussed the second honeymoon.

"We've spent all our cash on the party, so we're not going overboard," Nancy said. "Bill cashed in an old insurance policy, which was wonderful as it covered the whole event, but we kept a little bit aside for two days in London. We're going to see a show and everything!"

Nancy was like a giddy young girl.

When Louisa heard the front door bang, several minutes later, she felt a tremor of nerves knowing it was Bill and that the moment had arrived. Mari met her eye and nodded discreetly, as if agreeing with Louisa's thoughts that she would have to reveal her news.

Bill joined them at the dining table, saying: "She'd been here since half past three! I thought she'd never leave."

Louisa cleared her throat and pulled out the scan pictures from her hand bag. She held them against her chest and cleared her throat nervously a few more times.

Nancy stared at her daughter with a frown of confusion. She waited, knowing Louisa was about to speak.

"Mum, dad, I have something to tell you," said Louisa with determination, looking at the floor.

Nancy looked closely at the shiny film paper in Louisa's hand and placed her hand over her mouth in shock.

"Is that what I think it is?" Nancy asked.

Louisa began to weep and nodded her head. She handed the pictures to her mother.

Bill looked across at the scan images and exclaimed: "Bloody hell! What... who....?"

His face was blank. Louisa couldn't tell what her parents were thinking.

Nancy stepped forward with her arms outstretched and held her daughter tightly. Without letting go, she said: "How long have you known?"

"A few weeks", Louisa said, thinking it would sound better than a couple of months.

"How did this..." Nancy stammered. "I mean, I know *how* this happens, but..."

Nancy suddenly drew a sharp intake of breath as she realised something.

"Have you told Justin?" Bill said quietly, still in shock.

"Why would I tell Justin?" Louisa asked, astonished.

Nancy turned to Bill as he, too, realised.

"Blimey," was all that Bill could say. "It's the... other man's."

"His name is Chati," said Louisa defensively. "And he's coming to Scotland to see me. We're keeping in touch."

Nancy was looking at the scan pictures closely, her face of shock softening into a smile.

"Bill, look," she said, handing him the pictures.

Bill had one hand on his forehead as he examined the pictures. Suddenly, he looked up at

Louisa and said in a breathy voice: "This is our grandchild?"

"Yes," said Louisa, through tears.

Bill gave his daughter a tight hug.

"We're here for you," he said gently, his eyes welling up. "You know that. We can get that room ready for you."

"No, I won't need it," said Louisa confidently. "I'm going to stay with Mari."

Nancy looked at Mari with worry. "You don't have to do that," she said.

Louisa felt a small stab of insult but Mari put an arm around her and said: "I want her to stay. She's got her business up and running, so she can pay for certain things. Besides, I would miss her... and I'm going to be an auntie!"

Nancy took a photo of the scan pictures on her phone and asked if she could tell people, which Louisa said she could. "There's no point in hiding it," was what she had said. "It's going to be pretty obvious soon."

Louisa felt relieved and shaken at the same time. It was good to rid herself of secrets.

Nancy and Bill had taken the news as well as she could have hoped. When the sisters left for home, their parents were smiling. That was what Louisa had needed to see.

Mari took a slight detour to stop the car at Findhorn Bay on the way home. Nancy had always said this was the most beautiful bay in the world. Those words were hollow to children's ears, but as adolescence arrived and the world took on more colour and meaning, Mari and Louisa grew to share their mother's opinion on this majestic spot. The sisters got out of the car and sat on a bench at the water's edge, listening to the gentle ripple of the sea on the pebbles. Row boats and small yachts bobbed to the gentle beat of the ocean and the calm water in this sheltered bay reflected the peach-coloured evening sky. They said not a word as they absorbed their surroundings.

Eventually Mari said: "When I die, just scatter me here. This is the most peaceful, uplifting place I know."

"OK," said Louisa with a surprised laugh. "Can I build a sandcastle out of you first?"

Mari pulled an exaggerated comedy frown and held her sister's hand.

"No."

CHAPTER THIRTY-SEVEN

Louisa's lower abdomen felt tight with the very beginnings of a baby bump. She was now longing for a rounded tummy, just to reassure her things were progressing nicely. She felt like a fraud with a flat stomach, so as soon as she began to swell she wore tight dresses to show off her pregnant status.

It was a Thursday and Chati was flying into Inverness airport. They agreed it would be too strange for Louisa to greet him at arrivals and decided, instead, to meet the next morning, giving Chati a chance to sleep after the long journey.

Louisa kept glancing at the clock. At 3pm she looked up from her sewing machine to realise that her lover, of sorts, was finally in the same country.

In bed that night, she could barely settle to sleep knowing that he was in a hotel bed only minutes from where she lay.

What if we are both disappointed with each other in the harsh Scottish light, she wondered. *What if the sunshine turned us into different people? And what if we were only attracted to each other because it was forbidden? What does he hope for?*

The questions continued long into the night until, eventually, Louisa drifted into a light slumber.

When she awoke at 5am, her first thought was *what if he's a psycho?*

The next day, the meeting point was a coffee shop in the city centre. The time was 1pm.

It was only fifteen minutes until they were due to be reunited and Louisa felt sick to the stomach. She tried deep breathing as she hung about beside a rail of dresses in a shop next to the cafe. She didn't want to be seen too early. Her tactic was to allow him time to arrive and then she would show up five minutes late, avoiding an awkward wait, or worse arriving at the same time.

"Are you OK there?" asked a shop assistant. She had been watching Louisa's deep breathing from afar.

"Yes," said Louisa, smiling. "I'm just nervous. I'm meeting someone soon."

"Blind date?" asked the assistant, grinning.

"Sort of," said Louisa weakly. She began to shake.

Five minutes to go. This is hellish., thought Louisa, glancing nervously at her watch.

The minutes ticked by ever so slowly on Louisa's watch, until she could hold off no longer.

She made for the shop door and the assistant called after her: "Good luck. I hope he's a hunk."

Louisa laughed politely but couldn't speak, she was full of fear.

She made her way into the cafe and stood at the entrance peering at all the faces at every table. Eventually, a man waved his hand about at the back of the room and Louisa recognised the dark hair and golden skin. Her stomach flipped as she walked forward shyly.

She was wearing a pair of tight black jeans, which sat under her growing belly nicely, a simple green blouse and a black rain mack with a belt. She wanted to appear sophisticated – like a capable mother-to-be.

Chati was wearing a smart navy jacket with a hood and jeans. He grinned and stood up to kiss her cheek.

"You look beautiful," he said, handing her a bunch of pink gerberas.

"Thanks," she mumbled as she undid her jacket.

It was all very strange for both of them.

Chati broke the ice by explaining he had no idea what to wear in Scotland so he had bought the jacket earlier that day as he was freezing.

Louisa laughed nervously and chatted about getting used to the mild weather.

He was just as handsome as she remembered. He didn't need the sun streaming down on him to be breathtaking, she thought.

Chati's calm demeanour instantly soothed Louisa and she began chatting freely, asking about his journey and the hotel.

Eventually the conversation steered around to the more weighty subject of future plans.

"I have no set plan," said Chati carefully. "I could look for a job in computing here, perhaps," he said, knowing his qualifications were sought after the world over. He nervously added: " I'll take your lead. I'm in no hurry. Wait and see."

Louisa felt at ease. She was happy right there in that moment, looking into Chati's eyes.

"I'm glad I got in touch," she said happily.

The pair were so overwhelmed by meeting they had forgotten to mention the baby. It took until 3pm, still perched at the cafe table to bring up the subject.

"Are you well with... everything?" Chati asked sensitively, gesturing towards Louisa's stomach.

"Oh, yes, thanks," she said, laughing. "It's all fine."

She handed him the scan pictures from her coat pocket.

Chati was silent as he gazed at the pictures. Finally he said, softly. "It's amazing. I just can't believe it."

"I didn't know if you would be happy about it or not," admitted Louisa. "I was shocked and scared at first. It took me a while to feel good about it."
"I was happy the minute I read your message," Chati said warmly. "We're meant to be."

CHAPTER THIRTY-EIGHT

Louisa and Chati were glued to each other since their first meeting on Friday. It was now Monday. They'd shared meals at several restaurants, lay on his hotel bed chatting, walked by the river and shopped for warm 'Scottish' clothes.

Mari was happy her sister was enjoying the reunion, but couldn't help feeling a little bitter that she no longer had a dinner buddy and was thrust back into a life of watching TV alone.

Louisa explained to Chati about her new business and that there were orders waiting to be completed. She told him she needed all of Monday and Tuesday to work, but would see him for a drink at his hotel in the evenings. He agreed, happily. He would take whatever time he could get with Louisa. He would treat his free hours as a holiday, sight-seeing in Inverness.

Mari snuck into Louisa's bedroom before work on Monday morning.

"Well? How is it going?" she asked, excitedly. "I've hardly seen you."

Louisa sat up in bed and grinned.

"It's as though we've known each other forever," she said. "That sounds really cheesy, doesn't it?"

"Yeah," said Mari, chuckling. "That's fantastic though. I'm really happy for you."

After a pause, Mari whispered dramatically: "Have you been all over each other?"

Louisa tittered and said: "Strangely not. It's all we did in Dubai, but we haven't had the right moment yet. Is that odd?"

Mari looked surprised, but said: "No. It's probably a good thing. At least sex isn't the only thing you have in common."

She paused before asking: "Do you think he's going to live here? Will you be moving in together?"

"Steady on," said Louisa. "I don't want to push things."

She looked at Mari suspiciously and asked: "Do you want rid of me?"

"No, not at all," exclaimed Mari. "Quite the opposite. Although, I know it's inevitable that you'll move out if you and Chati make a go of it."

Mari looked crestfallen and Louisa suddenly felt protective.

"Let's not think about that yet," she said. "Anyway, I need to ask you a favour."

"What," asked Mari, curiously.

"I need a model..." said Louisa, hopefully, pointing towards a deep purple corset with a long train.

"No way," insisted Mari.

"It's just for the website," Louisa said, with a pleading tone. "My gut is expanding, so I don't want to squash it into a tight corset. Plus, that is actually your exact size. I need you."

Mari sighed. "I'll think about it," she said.

"Tonight? After work?" Louisa asked.

***

Louisa bought a bottle of sparkling wine and a box of chocolates for her sister and laid them on top of the purple burlesque costume on Mari's bed.

When Mari returned from work and went to change out of her smart clothes, she laughed to see the tempting bed display and shouted: "Louisa! OK, I accept the bribery."

Mari held the costume in the crook of her arm and went to the kitchen to fetch a two wine glasses. She poured a comic two centimetres, a mere token gesture into one glass for Louisa, adding a generous splash of raspberry sparkling water, and filled the second to the brim with wine. It was her first alcoholic drink since the burlesque night, a reassuring sign that she could take it or leave it.

She took the drinks through to Louisa's room and said she would be back in five minutes, rolling her eyes.

Louisa put on some electro swing music to set the scene of sassiness and sat cross-legged on the bed excitedly waiting for her sister to return.

Mari pushed the door an inch and said through the crack: "Are you ready? Don't laugh."

218

"Of course I won't laugh," retorted Louisa. "I made the blooming thing."

Mari entered, looking curvaceous and seductive, but holding herself weakly, as if hunching her shoulders would hide her physique.

"Right, we have a few things to sort out," insisted Louisa, standing up.

She grabbed a handful of hair slides and began tweaking and teasing Mari's hair. She pinned parts up for height at the crown and left other strands dangling on the nape of Mari's neck.

Louisa reached next for her make-up bag and quickly smeared some smoky grey eye shadow on Mari's lids before drawing on the customary red lippy.

"There," said Louisa standing back in admiration. "One more thing!"

Louisa pulled out a string of fake pearls from her top drawer and wrapped them twice around Mari's neck.

"I feel like a drag queen," moaned Mari.

"You look fantastic," said Louisa, pulling Mari's limbs gently into position. She handed Mari the wine and said: "Down it."

Mari did as she was told. In three huge gulps, her glass was drained.

Louisa turned up the volume of the music. Why Don't You by Gramophonedzie was playing.

"Is this a dance version of the song Jessica Rabbit sang?" asked Mari keenly.

"Yes," said Louisa, fully focused on her model. "Put your hand on your hip like this," she instructed.

"I love it," said Mari, suddenly taking on a different character. She held her bones elegantly, aware of the warm aftermath of the wine flowing through her.

Louisa took several pictures, before saying: "We need a different position. Would you feel brave enough to sit on the bed in a vintage vixen way?"

Mari gave it a go. Louisa moved Mari's legs until she was satisfied with the way they were elegantly curled behind her. Mari leaned forward on one arm and was instructed to look wistfully at the curtains as though they had been insulting her.

Mari laughed, but managed to get into the zone.

Damn you, curtains, she thought, frowning, before erupting into giggles.

Louisa was delighted with several of the photos and promised to show Mari once she had edited them.

"I want to see them *before* they appear on your website," Mari insisted.

Louisa snatched up her bag and coat, kissed her sister on the cheek and said she was late for meeting Chati, she had to hurry.

Mari stood in Louisa's room, fully tarted up and abandoned.

She strutted through to the kitchen to pour another wine and took it through to her bedroom to change into pyjamas for an early night.

The mirror distracted her, however, and a further twenty minutes was spent pulling seductive poses and looking in awe at her reflection.

I'm not bad, she thought. *I should do this sometime for a man. Dress up and knock him dead. Well, not literally dead, because then I'd be single all over again.*

CHAPTER THIRTY-NINE

Louisa and Chati were eating a takeaway in his hotel room.

"When can I meet your sister?" he asked. "I've been here for two weeks."

Louisa thought for a moment and said: "Tomorrow? Let's ask her out for dinner."

She was wearing a pair of fluffy pyjamas and had just got out of a warm, bubble bath in the en-suite. She had spent a few nights in Chati's bed so far. They were growing more comfortable each day.

A week after Chati's arrival was when things had turned from deep talk to deep passion. They'd been for a long walk and were resting in his room. Chati had his hand on Louisa's stomach affectionately when he planted his first gentle kiss on her neck. The familiar electric shock impulses surged through Louisa and she remembered how they got themselves into this situation in the first place. They were desperately attracted to each other, like two strong magnets being held opposite each other, just waiting to let go and smack into each other with force.

They made love as if they had been starved of it and were finally allowed to feast.

Another week later and here they were spending time together every day, but hiding away in hotel rooms and cafes.

"I don't want to rush things," said Chati, "but if I'm going to be staying here, maybe I should look for somewhere more permanent, rather than waste all my money on a hotel."

Louisa felt nervous, but realised they would need to formulate a plan.

"OK," she said, putting her arms around his neck. "Do you want to stay here?"

"Yes," he replied.

Louisa could feel tears welling in the corners of her eyes. "Are we officially together?"

Chati held her face and said: "I hope so."

They kissed, as if signing the contract.

Chati said he would begin a job and flat search the next day, giving Louisa time to finish some more orders. They said good night happily, falling asleep in each other's arms, in the warm glow of hope.

CHAPTER FORTY

The delicious scent of bacon drifted down the hallway into Mari's bedroom as she pulled on her tights. It was a work day. That usually meant shovelling down a rushed bowl of muesli for breakfast, not biting into juicy bacon.

She pulled on her skirt and followed the tempting smell expectantly.

Louisa was carefully folding rashers into a roll when she heard the kitchen door open and turned to give her sister a rapturous smile.

Something was up.

"Morning," Louisa said breezily, but with an undertone of nerves, which didn't go unnoticed by her sister.

"Morning," Mari responded, eyeing the situation for clues.

"I made you bacon," said Louisa, moving round to the table and gesturing for Mari to sit.

"Why?"

"If by that you mean 'thanks' then you're welcome," Louisa said quickly.

"Yes, thank you, my dear sister," responded Mari with sarcasm, "but *why*?"

"Does there have to be a motive?" Louisa asked, avoiding eye contact. She sat opposite Mari, who was now tucking into the warm roll.

"Oh, it's gorgeous anyway, I'm not complaining," Mari said with a mouth full.

Louisa smiled anxiously and watched her sister eat. She glanced at the clock and shifted in her seat. She put one hand in her pocket and took out a small piece of card.

"What's that?" Mari asked, still on high alert.

"This, well, it's something I wanted to show you," answered Louisa, still gripping the folded card close to her.

"Go on then," mumbled Mari. "Let me see."

Louisa carefully unfolded what Mari could now see what a flyer. Louisa examined it with a wry smile.

Mari placed her half-eaten roll on the plate impatiently. "What is it?"

Louisa laid it on the table and smoothed out the fold as best she could then rotated it to Mari's view. There, on the flier entitled Highland Seduction, was a picture of Mari fully trussed up in corset and lace.

"Holy shit!" she exclaimed with horror and hid her eyes with her hands. "Why didn't you tell me? Who's seen this? What is it for?"

"I didn't know until it came in the post yesterday," said Louisa quickly, placing one hand desperately over Mari's hand. She was trying to stifle a grin, but the faux expression of concern was not strong enough to overpower her excitement and her face ended up twisted into a sinister grimace.

"I got an email last week asking me to exhibit a few garments at a fashion event up north soon at some lavish castle and I snapped up the chance," explained Louisa, desperately stating her case. "They asked if they could use a few pictures from my website for promotional purposes, and, naturally, I said yes. I didn't expect..... *that*."

Both sisters eyed the card silently for a few moments.

Mari cleared her throat, straightened her back and considered her words carefully.

"I'm pleased for you," she said calmly. "I just..."

"I know it's a shock," said Louisa with an apologetic expression. "You have to admit you look amazing."

Mari's furrowed brow softened a little. "Well..... it doesn't look like me," she said, finally picking up the card.

"Yes it does," said Louisa with a smile. "That IS you. Start believing it."

The cleavage, the curve of her thighs, the confident expression.... they were there in print. It was definitely her, but not the version of herself she knew. Mari felt a kick of fear. These were unknown waters.

She exhaled slowly, realising her breath had been shallow all this time.

"So. Wow," Mari said looking deep into her sisters eyes. "You're going to have models strutting their stuff in your work."

"Not exactly," said Louisa, suddenly uncomfortable again.

"What do you mean?"

"They have a very small budget. They are simply providing a showcase for local designers to bring their own.... things," said Louisa cautiously, looking at the table.

"So what's your plan?"

"Well, obviously *I* can't model lingerie," said Louisa pointing at the blossoming baby bump.

The sentence hung in the air, unfinished. After a few awkward, silent moments, Mari offered the words: "That's a shame. I'm sure you'll work something out."

Suddenly, Mari could sense pleading in Louisa's eyes. It all fell into place like a punch in the gut. The bacon roll had been a ruse. She had backed her sister into a corner with a meaty bribe.

"No way in hell are you roping me into this," said Mari, suddenly rising from her chair. "The pictures were enough."

"Please Mar," said Louisa, looking crestfallen and desperate. "I don't have anyone else to ask, not anyone that would look like *that* in the pieces," she added as she motioned toward the flyer. "Think how good you felt that night we took the photos. I saw it in you. You changed when you put that bodice on and we had the music going. You became a Mari I've never seen before. This could be good for you. Seriously."

Mari felt her insides flutter and lurch as though a miniature gymnastics troupe had entered her gut and were going for the gold medal. She felt ill.

"I can't Louisa. I'm not... I'm not you."

***

Mari couldn't shake the words Highland Seduction from her mind for the rest of the morning. The gastro-gymnastics wouldn't piss off either.

Why am I wasting my thoughts on this? She asked herself as she attempted to concentrate on her work. *I've already said no. It's not my kind of thing. Where the hell is my chocolate?*

She rummaged in the top drawer of her desk. Not there. She slammed it shut and began a raid mission on the second drawer before slamming it shut too. Mari looked up to see her four colleagues in the shared office frowning at all the noise she was making.

"Has anyone seen a big bar of fruit and nut?" she asked. "One of those huge ones – you know, the ones you're supposed to share but, I mean, as if. Share with my Jekyll side maybe!" she added nervously, hoping for a laugh.

"No. No-one has seen your enormous bar of chocolate," was the only response she got as they all refocused on their computer screens.

You shouldn't be eating it anyway, Mari scolded herself. *Not if you're supposed to look good in.... what? Why am I thinking about bloody corsets? Mari, don't give in. Yes, she's your poor pregnant little sister who's struggling to get her business off the ground, but..... Oh for god's sake.*

Mari picked up her phone and typed out the text: Fine. I'm not happy about this, but I said I would support you with this business, so I will. Argh. What have you turned me into sis? X

CHAPTER FORTY-ONE

"Come on Mar," Louisa barked with frustration. "Let your inner seductress out. You look so stiff it's uncomfortable to watch."

Mari was wearing a basque, stockings and high heels and reluctantly shuffling down the hallway in the flat to Louisa's orders.

"Maybe this is the worst idea you've ever had," she said, with tears welling in her eyes.

"I'm sorry," said Louisa with sudden panic. "It's just.... you're holding back too much. I don't get it."

"You never will," said Mari, gulping her emotions back down before they fully erupted. "I've never done anything like this. I'm background girl, not 'tart me up and parade me' girl."

Louisa looked insulted. "It's classy. Not tarty."

Mari smiled, apologetically. She gave Louisa a hug, having to lean further forward due to the bump between them.

"It's not as if I wouldn't swap places with you if I could," said Louisa with a feint hint of bitterness.

"I know," said Mari, feeling a stab of guilt. "OK. I need to suck it up and be brave. For you."

"Don't just do it for me," said Louisa. "Do it for you."

Mari sighed, held her head high and tried again.

"That's a *little* better," said Louisa, smiling encouragingly. "Remember, we need to work on a big burlesque finish. I want people to remember my outfits."

"One thing at a time," warned Mari. "I'll watch that list of video clips you gave me. I promise."

"Thank you," said Louisa, glancing at her watch. "Oh! I'd better go."

"Chati?" asked Mari, not really needing an answer.

"Yeah," said Louisa feeling guilty, then chastising herself for feeling that way. Surely she could divide her time between her sister and the father of her baby without feeling bad about it. Besides, he had some property schedules to show her. Not that she would breathe a word of this to Mari. Not right now, anyway.

Louisa grabbed her coat and dashed off, leaving Mari to practice some moves alone.

"I can do this," she said, in the hope that hearing the words out loud might somehow make them true. "Yeah. I can fake it for *one night*."

CHAPTER FORTY-TWO

Louisa stood nervously in the lobby of Greenglen Castle, surrounded by gorgeous girls in various states of attire. Some donned quirky dresses made from tweed and others were balancing beneath elaborate, towering hair styles incorporating wild heather and thistles. It was all very sexy and very Scottish. Louisa had never been a part of anything like this before. She felt the nerves of hope stirring, as she realised this could be a springboard to greater things.

She knew Mari was suffering in the lounge-turned-dressing room. But she also knew what Mari was capable of, even if Mari herself didn't fully believe it. All Louisa could do now was watch from beneath the enormous chandelier in the lobby as each model took her turn to enter the sumptuous ball room full of fashion and media folk, as well as charity representatives, and people who were just there for the bubbly and nibbles. A photographer's flash flickered like lightning each time a new girl entered the room and Louisa looked on nervously as each model disappeared from her view and into the gaze of dozens of eyes.

From behind, Louisa heard a man's voice bellow: "Legs Eleven!"

She turned to see a tall man in designer glasses with diamante ear studs, holding his arms out to hug her.

"That's me," she said chirpily, as his arms fell heavily around her. "And you are...?"

"It's me, Andy Adrenaline," he said, holding Louisa's shoulders firmly. "Of course you won't recognise me in my male disguise."

She gave a great cry of joy and finally reciprocated the embrace. "Oh my gosh, I would never have recognised you without the wig and make-up... and lingerie. How are you?"

"I'm fab," he said grinning. "I saw the ad for this and just had to come to see what mischief you've been up to."

His eyes fell on the bump. One eyebrow arched dramatically and Louisa laughed: "Don't ask."

"I don't need to, honey."

"Thank you for coming anyway," she said, laughing. "It's good to see you – the other you! I'll catch you after."

Finally, Mari joined the lobby girls, fully made up and looking every bit as beautiful as the others around her. She grabbed a glass of bubbly from a passing tray, startling the young man who was carrying it, and downed it in one.

"Careful," said Louisa protectively. "You can as much as you want drink after."

Mari hadn't been aware her sister was watching. "Dutch courage," she said with a shaky voice.

The opening bars of an upbeat Caravan Palace track began and Louisa knew this was Mari's cue. She had chosen the song by the quirky electro swing band, knowing it wasn't too sexy for Mari but had an upbeat vintage vibe, which she hoped was infectious enough to persuade her sister to enjoy the moment.

Mari gripped Louisa's hand nervously, before Louisa gave her a supportive pat on the back and whispered: "You're amazing."

Mari made for the entrance.

Louisa ran through the hall to the door at the back of the ball room, desperate to see what her sister would do. She slipped in through a crowd of people and watched as Mari walked to the start of a long runway, which ran between tables full of people drinking, their eyes all on Mari.

Mari's face was serious.

Come on, loosen up girl, thought Louisa more nervous than she had been on her own burlesque evening.

Mari forced a smile and began to walk quickly down the pathway, her chiffon train gliding behind her fishnet thighs.

What's she doing? Where's the twirl we practiced?

Mari was freestyling. She had forgotten the routine. Louisa watched on, her hands clasped together anxiously. She felt her hopes crash as Mari missed another important move. Mari reached the end of the runway too quickly, having cut out all her planned manoeuvres. Thinking on her feet, she weaved her way

234

past the first table and pulled off a satin glove, launching it in the air before it landed on the shoulder of a mesmerised man innocently sipping his pint. He spluttered with glee as Mari tousled his hair.

What the....? Louisa watched curiously, her fear melting into intrigue.

Mari tossed the other glove backwards over her shoulder with a flirtatious smile and made her way straight for a middle-aged man in a grey suit. She tripped over a Chanel handbag and bumped down on his lap. With one arm draped around his neck she prized the glass of champagne from his fingers and downed it in one before rising up and giving him a wink and a wave.

Some guys from the back of the room wolf-whistled and a few other tables hooted and clapped.

Mari was in her stride.

Louisa clasped her hand over her mouth in disbelief, stifling a giggle. *She is nailing this. My so-called shy, reserved sister has this room in a trance!*

Running out of ideas and desperate to make her way back to the exit, Mari wound her way seductively through some more tables, one hand on her hip, and headed back up the runway. At the top, she paused to strike a pose and tear off her train, knowing that was the one move Louisa was desperate for her to execute. She tossed the feather-light piece of fabric into the audience and a young woman caught it gleefully and swirled it around her head like a lasso, to great cheers from her friends.

Mari made her exit and held onto a large, oak desk in the lobby for support, as she caught her breath. Louisa ran back through the hallway, clutching her tummy, to find her sister. Mari looked shell-shocked. Louisa was brimming with joy.

"You did it! You did it! Thank you!" Louisa gushed, holding her sisters hands and practically springing around.

"I did," said Mari with wide eyes. "I actually bloody did. Thank *you* Louisa."

The sisters stood there, hand in hand in that decadent castle, aware of the changes that were brewing within them. Their moment was broken abruptly when one of the event organisers burst between them announcing "I need a selfie with the Legs Eleven sisters."

Louisa flashed a self-assured smile for the camera as crowds of impressed fashion students began to swarm.

This is the validation she's been longing for, thought Mari watching her sister fondly. Her Legs Eleven sister.

CHAPTER FORTY-THREE

It was the week before Bill and Nancy's second wedding.

Louisa and Mari were having lunch at the flat with Nancy, who was visiting to see the sisters in their purple dresses. She also wanted to give them jewellery as gifts to wear on the day.

"Look at that little bump of yours," said Nancy, eyeing Louisa's tummy. "It's so cute."

Louisa rubbed it affectionately. "I can feel it wriggling now," she said.

Mari added: "One night she had me sitting with my hand on it for about twenty minutes until I finally felt a little kick. It was amazing."

"Your dad and I want to take you pram shopping soon," said Nancy with glee. "I have to admit, I've already bought a few blankets."

Louisa was delighted to be able to speak so positively about what once felt like a curse.

"When can we meet your man, then?" asked Nancy.

She hadn't told her mother very much about how things were progressing with Chati, but she had explained they were together.

"That was something I was going to ask you actually," said Louisa shyly. "I wondered if he should come next week, so he can meet everyone at once. Only if it wouldn't ruin your seating plans and cost too much extra," she added with embarrassment.

"Of course," Nancy said thoughtfully, but added after a pause: "I think I should meet him before everybody else though. I am the grandmother of his child, after all. Phone him and ask him to come here."

"What, now?" asked Louisa.

"Yes. He should make that effort for his baby's granny, should he not?" replied Nancy.

Mari gulped, nervously. She had met Chati one night at Pizza Hut. She liked him very much. He was polite, well spoken and clearly adored Louisa. She knew Nancy would like him, she just hoped Nancy wouldn't frighten him with forcefulness.

This could go either way, thought Mari. *Mum will either give him a faux iron lady treatment, demanding respect from him, or she will smother him with instant love.*

Louisa took her mobile through to the bedroom to call Chati.

"Hi," she said when he picked up. "Mum wants you to meet her. Now."

He hurried over, conscious of making a good impression, stopping for flowers on the way.

When he arrived at the flat and handed the flowers to Nancy, she was instantly charmed and proceeded to grill the man about his future with her daughter.

"He's very handsome," Nancy gushed to Louisa, as if he couldn't hear.

"What are you doing for work?" she asked. "I've actually got an interview for a job as a computing lecturer at the college next week," he said, which impressed Nancy. "It's a start," he said modestly.

"Lovely," she commented. "And where will you live?"

Louisa shot her mother a disapproving look. Nancy was digging too quickly. Louisa had planned to slowly filter these details out over the coming months, not all in one like shoving a three course meal into a take-away bucket.

Chati looked at Louisa for approval. She glanced down at the table awkwardly.

He told Nancy he'd just paid a rental deposit on a flat in the suburbs of Inverness.

"It's a very nice place," he insisted. "It'll do until I settle into my job. There's a garden for when the baby's walking."

Mari grew hot with frustration. *What else don't I know?* she wondered.

"Are you moving in," she asked Louisa abruptly.

Louisa stiffened. She hesitated, then said: "Well, yes, I will be... at some point."

She felt caught in a trap. She couldn't hurt Chati by playing this down after all the effort he had made to set this up. She also longed to be with him and wanted this home life secured in time for the birth. However, she knew it would hurt Mari to think there were secret plans, after all the support she had given.

Nancy's eyebrows rose with surprise and she said: "You're a secretive girl, aren't you," to Louisa. "But I'm really pleased for you. It only makes sense to do all this now before the baby comes."

She added, warmly: "I can see you two will be happy together."

They both smiled and looked at each other.

Mari said nothing. She avoided Louisa's eye contact.

***

The next morning Louisa found an opportunity to talk to Mari.

"Hi Mar," she said, pushing Mari's bedroom door open gently. "I hope you're not upset I never told you about the flat. I just wanted to take everything really slowly. I haven't decided when to move in. I suppose I'm a bit scared."

Mari was sitting on the edge of the bed applying her make-up. She put the lid on her mascara tube and looked at Louisa.

"I'm happy for you," she said sadly. "I suppose I'm just feeling sorry for myself because I'm going to miss you when you go."

Louisa sat down on the bed next to her.

"I'm sorry," she said, trying not to cry. "You've been so supportive."

Mari was crying, which prompted Louisa's tears to burst their banks.

"We're always crying these days," joked Mari. "It's all your fault."

They laughed through the tears.

"I'll be OK," Mari said. "You need to do this. You need to build a home with Chati. It's going to be amazing."

"And at least it's only a small journey for you to come and see the baby," added Louisa. "We'll still be in the same town."

"Yes, that's true," said Mari. "I can take it here for sleepovers when you want date nights."

They smiled sighed, before Louisa returned to her sewing station.

Mari would miss the clicking and loud vibrating noises coming from the sewing machine.

CHAPTER FORTY-FOUR

Bill stood at the grand double doors of the Old Moray Hotel greeting the friends and relatives as they arrived.

His brother, Pete, brought a dram through from the bar. "Get that whisky in you. It'll calm your nerves," he said, patting Bill on the back.

"I feel like a 22-year-old groom all over again," Bill said anxiously.

"You must be nuts, going through all this flowery shit again, Bill," teased his oldest friend Derek.

Bill laughed and nodded his head. "It's all for Nance," he said.

Fran tumbled out of a taxi directly in front of the hotel steps. It was clear she had been drinking.

"Bill!" she cried. "I'm not late am I?"

"No, it's only half past one," said Bill, coldly.

"Ooh, who is this handsome young man?" Fran asked stroking Chati's tie.

Bill had forgotten Nancy tasked him with "looking after" Chati.

"He won't know anybody, so be nice to him," Nancy had warned Bill the previous evening. "He's come all the way to Scotland to look after our daughter. How romantic."

Bill quickly put a protective arm over Chati's shoulder and said in an official tone: "This is Louisa's man."

"Oh," said Fran giggling for no apparent reason, other than chardonnay. "Lucky woman. Is it you who got her up the duff?"

"Fran!" said Bill abruptly."There's a drink inside with your name on it."

With that, Fran shuffled in on her high heels to find a free drink in the lobby. She proceeded to mingle, joining various groups' conversations, uninvited.

Two o'clock eventually arrived and everyone made their way through to a bright ceremony room laden with purple pansies and hyacinths.

A string quartet played gently in the corner as Bill stood nervously at the front. The small gathering of people found their seats, with Bill pointing to one on the front row for Chati, who was wandering around like a lost lamb.

The ceremony leader announced the arrival of today's "leading lady" and Nancy entered looking glorious, head to toe in varying shades of purple. On her head she wore a large fascinator decorated with feathers.

Behind her, Mari and Louisa walked elegantly in their floor-length gowns, Louisa's bulging slightly at the belly. She was aware of whispers from relatives who had only been told that morning about her pregnancy. They were intrigued to see her mystery man at the front, too.

Louisa didn't care what anyone had to say. She knew she was on the right path. She caught Chati's eye as the three women reached the top of the aisle and felt a surge of excitement.

Mari and Louisa stood to the side, to allow the friends and family to view Nancy and Bill read new vows to each other.

Hankies were passed around to mop up tears of joy as Nancy vowed to continue to wash Bill's socks and pretend to listen to football results as long as they both shall live. Bill promised to love her through experimental cooking and extreme decorating until death do they part.

Their humorous readings sent ripples of laughter around the room, but it was clear to see that these two were deeply in love, joking aside.

After the couple ceremoniously cut a large cake in the shape of a flower, everyone settled at several tables to a hot buffet meal.

After the meal, Bill stood up to say a few words.

"I would just like to say thank you all for coming today, it means so much to Nancy and I," he began. "As you will know, I had a near death experience this year and it put a lot of things into perspective. It reminded me that the things I value most are my beautiful daughters and my wife, Nancy, who I couldn't be without. I won't go on and on. I would just like us all to raise our glasses to Nancy."

Everyone raised their drinks and said in unison: "To Nancy."

"There's one more thing, before I sit down," Bill added. "I'd like everyone to welcome Chati, who has come a long way across the world to be with my daughter. I am very grateful to him for bringing her happiness."

The diners raised their glasses and said in scattered timing: "To Chati."

He blushed and gave a small wave. Louisa's heart swelled with pride and she blew her father a kiss.

Bill sat down and chatter commenced around the tables.

Fran, who was sitting opposite Louisa, stood up and began to chime her glass with a spoon. Nancy groaned as everyone silenced to listen to her sister.

"Congratulations to Nancy and Bill," she said with a slight slur. "To me, after all these years, Bill as is much family to me as my sister is. I have known him longer than I knew the pre-Bill Nancy, if that makes sense."

Everyone smiled and glanced at Bill, who was grinning with gritted teeth, fearing what may come.

"They are the best couple I know," Fran continued. "I don't believe there are skeletons in their closets, which is rare in such a long relationship. Most people have had affairs or gone to swinging parties by their stage. Maybe they have! We don't know... Anyway, I give you both my warmest wishes and hope for many more loving years for you both."

Nancy smiled and began to clap gently.

"I don't envy you, however," Fran continued, putting paid to the ripple of applause circulating the room. "Some might assume I am lonely because I don't have a Bill. I haven't had a family of my own..."

The relatives all began to look at their napkins and shuffle nervously in their seats.

"But I am quite happy, I can assure you. You don't need a man to be happy. Well, maybe you need *that* man to be happy (she pointed at Chati), eh Louisa? Hot stuff indeed."

Nancy rose from her chair and said abruptly, but without malice: "Thank you so much Fran. That was lovely. We've run out of time for speeches."

The relief around the table was obvious.

Fran sat back down, tutting with disapproval. She had a great monologue prepared about finding peace in her soul and accepting her solo existence. She was going to explain about her therapy sessions and the management of her only real relationship, which was with booze. She was most annoyed that Nancy had cut this short.

Louisa had pre-warned Chati about her aunt so he handled the embarrassment with grace.

Mari was giggling into her napkin, pretending she was having a coughing fit, but she caught Louisa's eye and was rumbled. Louisa smirked and mouthed: "not funny," but she broke into a small laugh.

Nancy turned to Bill and said: "That went OK. It could have been a lot worse." He nodded in agreement.

The tables were cleared from the room and a traditional Scottish band made their way to the back of the room.

Fiddles and accordions tore into action and people were swinging each other aggressively around the dance floor in an orderly manner with huge smiles across their faces.

It was like nothing Chati had ever seen before. Louisa dragged him up to dance. They spun around and jumped in time with everyone else and collapsed back on their chairs after only one song. Bill's friend Derek, who Mari and Louisa used to call Uncle Derek, tried will all his might to persuade Louisa to join him for an Eightsome Reel. Eventually he accepted her excuses as she patted her baby bump and he moved on to Mari, who had no way out. Mari mouthed "help me" as she was pulled up to dance her way around the entire floor with Derek gripping her arm a little too tightly.

Granny June bobbed daintily at the side of the dance floor with her walking stick, clearly delighted to see her family all around.

By 9pm auntie Fran was slumped in her seat asleep. Nancy ordered her a taxi and sent her home. She paid the driver extra cash to make sure she made it through the front door.

The whole day was a big success and Mari, Chati and Louisa went home with Nancy and Bill to drink cups of tea and eat leftover wedding cake before turning in for the night.

Nancy remarked how lovely it was to have everyone sleeping under one roof, "including this one," she said patting Louisa's tummy.

The next morning, Louisa awoke to find a plastic shopping bag leaning on the door of the spare bedroom. Inside it was Nancy's purple frock and a note saying: *Please turn this into one of your splendid burlesque costumes. Don't tell your dad. It will be a surprise! PS Send me the bill as if I was any other customer.*

Louisa laughed and tucked the bag discreetly into her holdall.

CHAPTER FORTY-FIVE

Nancy stirred hot porridge in a pan on the hob, while the others chatted around the dining table. It was the morning after the second wedding party.

Chati admitted he had never tried porridge

"The pressure's on, Nance," shouted Bill. "Make this the best batch you've ever done, otherwise the boy will might be put off for life."

Nancy placed a squeezy bottle of syrup and a bowl of blueberries in the middle of the table, ready for dressing the steaming bowls of porridge she placed in front of each person. She then sat down with her own bowl and began squeezing and scattering her toppings.

"This is lush," said Mari. "It's been ages since I've had this."

Chati said he liked it, but ate it very slowly using only the tip of his spoon. Nancy wasn't convinced. She rushed to the cupboard and brought out a packet of croissants. "I can warm some of these as well", she said, placing them on a baking tray. "Bill, get the butter and jam!"

Bill put his spoon in his bowl and rose to fetch the items, plus a few knives for spreading, while Nancy delivered a stack of plates "for anyone who wants one".

The family ate the hearty breakfast, making small talk about their plans for the day. Mari was going shopping, Louisa and Chati were just going to go for a walk and Bill thought he might manage a round of golf.

Nancy wanted to clean the house listening to Barbara Streisand and then catch up on some TV dramas she had recorded.

"We'll have to pack our cases this afternoon," she said to Bill. "London is calling."

The phone rang and Nancy leapt to her feet and out into the hallway to answer it.

When she returned she was pale and moved as if she were wading through water. Without saying a word, she grasped for the back of her chair for support and made her way clumsily round to sit down.

"What on earth's the matter?" asked Bill.

"It's Fran," Nancy said, a little breathless. "She's dead."

The previous night Fran had been led by the arm into her house by the kindly taxi driver. He escorted her through to the living room, which was a mess of newspapers and piles of junk. He noticed a bucket next to Fran's arm chair in front of the telly and dreaded to think what that was for. Fran told him she wasn't an invalid, or a decrepit old woman, and that he could leave now. That was the last he saw of her.

What happened when the taxi driver left was known only to Fran.

She kicked a few shopping bags full of balls of wool – she had been determined to knit a cardigan, but never got round to it – away from the chunky dated music system and pressed play. Bruce Springsteen blasted out from the speakers as Fran poured herself a triple measure of dark rum from the shelving unit next to her arm chair.

Nancy hadn't been in Fran's house for a year. She would have been furious to see the state it was in. Fran had begun visiting Nancy at home more frequently in the hope it would prevent her from coming here.

You really don't need this drink, Fran thought as she took a sip. *You've had enough at the wedding. Wedding! It wasn't a bloody wedding. They were at it! Hoping for presents, I'll bet. They're already married. Idiots.*

Despite her self-appointed advice to stop drinking, she continued.

It had been three weeks since she last attended the alcoholics support group. She had taken a severe dislike to a woman who was a regular at the group, who had insisted Fran go tee-total or stop coming.

"You're bringing us down," said the woman to Nancy. "We have to sit here, smelling the booze off you and listening to your stupid ideas about how you can control your drinking when you can't!"

Fran gave her two fingers, upped and left.

Since then the most productive thing she had done was food shopping. She managed to bathe and dress herself smartly for Nancy and Bill's party, but only because her 85-year-old mother had phoned to remind her.

That evening, Fran listened to her favourite songs, whilst drinking herself into a dizzy haze. She fell asleep, as she did most nights, in the arm chair, but this time, with a cushion behind her back her head rolled backwards. When the vomit volcano erupted, as it did regularly, hence the bucket, there was nowhere for it to go but down. She choked on her own vomit to Born in the USA.

CHAPTER FORTY-SIX

Nancy dissolved into a mess of guilt after the news of her sister's death.

"I should have done more for her," she cried hysterically at the dining table, as Bill put his arms around her. "I should have been checking up on her. She choked on her own vomit, for goodness sake!"

"That's not your fault," said Bill.

"But I could have left the party to take her home," said Nancy sobbing. "If I had put her to bed properly she might not have choked."

"You don't know that, Nance," said Bill, stroking her hair. "It could have happened any night. You know what she was like. She was out of your control."

"But they said her house was a real mess, I could have been more supportive," said Nancy.

It was the police who had phoned Nancy after the neighbours reported the Bruce Springsteen album had been on repeat for a few hours.

Mari, Louisa and Chati could sense Nancy needed space. They hugged her and left, saying they would phone later in the day. Mari offered to take the day off work the next day, to help with anything she could. Nancy appreciated this gesture and went for a long bath, to summon the strength to phone her mother.

In the early days, Fran was the favourite. She was an academic and excelled at school and university.

It was only in later life when Fran began to close herself off to life that she became unpleasant to be around. As each year passed, Fran grew increasingly bitter and isolated.

"I can't believe she's gone," said June, crying down the phone. "My daughter... taken before me."

It was an agonising phone call and Nancy hung up feeling wrung out.

The next day, Nancy embraced the necessities with Mari by her side. She turned the key to Fran's house and was hit by a smell of vomit and rotten food. The living room also had a faint smell of urine.

"It's disgusting in here," said Nancy, screwing up her face. "What the hell had she become? I had no idea it was this bad."

"I know," Mari agreed. "She always seemed clean enough when I saw her. You would never imagine this."

Nancy picked up a yellowed photo in a brass frame of Fran at her graduation. She looked healthy and full of hope.

"She looks a bit like you, Mari," said Nancy fondly.

"Yeah, I see what you mean," said Mari, with horror. She vowed never to become the next Fran. She would keep trying online dating and only drink on weekends. This was a slap in the face.

"It's so sad how someone can waste all that talent," said Nancy shaking her head sadly.

The funeral was held five days later in a large church in Elgin.

There weren't very many in attendance, as Fran had cut herself off from more and more people every year. She would insult old friends, just to get rid of them.

"I can't stand buying Christmas presents," she once said to Nancy, "so I just unfriend people."

She had coined her own phrase "unfriend" long before Facebook ever did.

Nancy had assumed her sister was joking about this, but looking around the barren church she realised it must have been true.

June sat at the front, sniffing into a hanky, while Nancy read aloud to the small gathering.

She paid tribute to her sister's intelligence and great qualifications and mentioned the fact that Fran liked dogs. There wasn't an awful lot more to say, being that she had never shown a real interest in the girls when they were children and had never travelled or had prominent relationships.

Fran was laid to rest in New Elgin cemetery.

The family had tea and sandwiches at a hotel, which Nancy insisted was not to be the Old Moray Hotel, as it would scar her beautiful memory of the second wedding.

As Nancy and Bill drove home she switched on the Radio only to hear Midnight from Cats. She hissed and switched it off quickly. Cats was the show they would have seen that week, had they gone on their second honeymoon.

CHAPTER FORTY-SEVEN

Mari lifted the sewing table from her work car and carried it into the ground floor flat which was swiftly becoming Louisa and Chati's family home.

Louisa had only spent one night there, but already there were bold art prints hanging in the living room and fluffy teal cushions on the rented sofa.

"Come and see the baby's room," Louisa said excitedly as she led Mari through to an empty box room.

"I'm sure it'll be lovely," said Mari, looking for a feature to remark upon.

The flat smelled clean and new. Chati had already bought a wooden cot and was in the process of building it on the living room floor when Mari arrived.

The three of them, Mari, Louisa and Chati, sat at the small kitchen table for coffee and bacon rolls, bought by Mari from the old snack van near Williamsons. She had seen Johnny's VW Golf parked near the furniture shop and lowered her head for fear of being seen.

Sitting with Louisa and Chati, gave Mari a good feeling. She no longer felt she was losing Louisa. With the wedding party and funeral she had seen the couple frequently over the past few weeks. She was getting to know her future brother-in-law - as she began calling him - quite well. She never felt unwelcome around them.

After they finished their tea, Louisa walked around the flat, holding her expanding tummy, as if it was a hand rest.

"This is going to be my sewing area," she said of a large corner of the master bedroom. "I'll have to keep the baby away from all the needles and scissors."

She went on to talk about the range of baby bedding and decor she had seen in Mothercare and Mari listened enthusiastically, picturing it all taking shape.

She left the flat with a positive feeling and went home for a long, hot bath and an early night.

Louisa and Chati lay quietly in their new home, clutching each other and feeling like the luckiest people alive.

CHAPTER FORTY-EIGHT

Louisa's bump was enormous. She hit several people on the back of the head with it as she squeezed along the row to find her seat next to Mari.

"We should have end seats," she said to her sister scornfully. "I constantly need to pee these days."

Mari rolled her eyes and said nothing. They were at a charity bingo night arranged by Mari's work colleagues. She hadn't spent enough time with Louisa lately and thought this would be a harmless, easy activity for a heavily pregnant woman. Mari hadn't banked on the continuous cycle of toilet breaks her sister would need.

It was one of those 'bring a party to a party' nights and there were several other work teams involved at different tables.

"I've never played bingo," said Louisa. "It's about time I did, with my business being named after a bingo number!"

"Eyes down," called the young man at the front. He was dressed in a multi-coloured waistcoat and was brimming with hyperactive enthusiasm.

He proceeded to call out numbers and Mari and Louisa desperately dabbed at their cards, failing to keep up to speed.

"Legs Eleven!" called the bingo man.

"That's me" joked Louisa, thrusting her arms in the air and giggling. Mari laughed so much she snorted, while serious players around them tutted and shushed the sisters.

During a break, Mari went to the bar and was standing next to someone she had spotted from her table earlier.

He was in his late thirties, with a neat beard and a strong build.

Now, he's a real man, thought Mari, comparing him to Johnny.

The young woman behind the bar looked at the man and then at Mari impatiently.

"Who's next?" she asked sourly.

The man turned to Mari with a smile and said: "Ladies first."

She thanked him and ordered some drinks.

Before she had a chance to think of something else to say another member of bar staff approached and took the man's order. Her moment had passed. Not wanting to wait around and look desperate, she took the drinks back to the table.

"That man at the bar is gorgeous," she said to Louisa, who began sizing him up. "Don't stare!"

Mari hardly dabbed any numbers during the remaining games as she could barely take her eyes off him two tables away. On three occasions he caught her looking and smiled.

"Give him your number," Louisa said forcefully. "You might never see him again."

"I can't do that," said Mari, but inside she was already planning how she would do it.

By the time she had formulated a plan and discussed with Louisa the pros and cons of taking the risk she looked up to see his chair was empty. He was gone.

Mari's spirit crumpled.

"Another one bites the dust," she muttered.

CHAPTER FORTY-NINE

At 2am Louisa sounded the alarm.

She called Nancy and Bill, as well as Mari, to tell them her waters had broken.

They all excitedly asked what they should do and were disappointed to be told "nothing".

"I'll call you again, when something else happens," she said before hanging up.

Nancy and Bill lay there in the darkness unable to sleep. They got out of bed and made hot chocolate, which they drank while watching recordings of Downton Abby.

Mari tossed and turned in bed, thinking of Louisa and wondering if she was in a lot of pain. She managed to get back to sleep after about an hour. She had been determined to sleep so she could save energy for when she was needed, or rather when she could hold the baby.

Louisa paced the bedroom, dripping amniotic fluid onto a pathway made of towels, while Chati phoned the hospital.

An hour later they were in the ward.

Louisa was checked over by the midwife on duty and everything was as it should be, but because her waters had broken she couldn't go home.

Chati held her hand and read her newspaper articles between contractions, which were gradually increasing.

Louisa took some mild painkillers and lay on a bed, fearing what was to come. Seven hours later, she thumped Chati on the thigh to wake him from his sleep as the pain was intensifying.

"I'm here, Louisa, I'm with you," said Chati sleepily.

"Stay awake, like I have to!" she snarled.

The contractions were rolling by more frequently and growing more intense. At 4pm she was yelling in pain and crying that it had to surely be over soon.

She breathed gas and air through a tube as if her life depended on it and worked through each contraction, listening to the calming advice of the midwife. She was disappointed not to have Carla for her labour. She would have hung on every word of Carla's with a feeling of security. Carla was a community midwife, however, and would see her on the other side, when the baby was at home.

The grand finale arrived at 10pm, with Louisa pushing with all her might and Chati feeling entirely helpless.

With one last great heave their daughter was born. She had a head full of fluffy black hair and a perfect, round, little nose.

Louisa wept with joy. She had no words. She touched every part of her tiny daughter and kissed Chati's hand. He stroked her back and wiped tears from his eyes.

"What are you going to call her?" asked the midwife.

"Cinderella," said Louisa.

The midwife's eyes grew wide with shock. She had heard all manner of names, but never a Disney Princess.

"I'm kidding," Louisa said. Then she looked into Chati's eyes, before saying: "Maria. It's close to my sister's name."

***

Mari raced to the hospital the next morning for visiting hours. She couldn't wait to get her hands on baby Maria.

She stopped at Mothercare on the way to buy a tiny tutu, a stuffed pink elephant and a stack of little babygros in bright, quirky patterns, knowing Louisa would adore them.

She met Nancy and Bill at the hospital entrance by chance, who were equally buzzing.

They made their way up to the third floor, laden with gifts and Nancy holding onto a giant pink helium balloon.

Chati met them at the ward door and was almost floored by hugs as they each congratulated him. He showed them the way to Louisa and Maria.

Louisa was sitting up in bed, wearing a pink dressing gown, holding her newborn daughter and wiping away tears of joy, induced by the sight of her excited family.

They each took turns at holding the youngest family member and describing her beauty.

After holding Maria and telling her gently that she was going to be the best auntie a girl could wish for, Mari left her parents to enjoy some time with their granddaughter, hugged Louisa and said she would be back for the evening visiting time.

The electronic voice announced that the elevator was arriving and the doors slid open slowly. Mari's heart skipped a beat to see bingo man.

She stepped in and pressed the ground floor button shyly.

"I know you, don't I?" he said.

"I'm not sure," Mari lied. She was able to recall the blue checked shirt and brown leather boots he had been wearing the other week, but she pretended not to.

"Bingo!" he said. They both laughed at the irony.

"What are you doing here?" he asked as the doors opened and they both stepped out.

"My sister just had a baby," Mari said.

"Mine too!" the man exclaimed. "Just last night. A boy."

They walked out to the car park together and lingered a little too long at the edge of the pavement, neither one wanting to leave.

"Will you be visiting later?" he asked.

"Yes," said Mari, with a flirtatious smile.

"I'll see you tonight then," he said, grinning.

Mari turned and walked to her car, a grin spreading across the width of her face. He would definitely be seeing her later. And again the next day. And the day after that.

If you liked this book and want to keep up with other work from the writer, please visit
www.pearlheartpublishing.co.uk
Or email **pearlheartpublishing@yahoo.com**

ABOUT THE AUTHOR:

Sarah May Fraser is a thirty-something journalist, writer and mother who lives in Moray, Scotland.
She graduated with a degree in journalism in 2004 and has since written for a huge range of publications including newspapers, magazines and books. This is her first novel (although she has been known to do a spot of fiction ghost writing- but that's top secret, of course).

Printed in Great Britain
by Amazon